I0682229

Boiling Point

The Breakup of the United States of America and its Citizens

by

Tom Merritt

Boiling Point

by Tom Merritt

Copyright © 1997 Tom Merritt, All rights reserved.

Revised edition Creative Commons © 2006 Tom Merritt

Printed in the United States of America

NOTES:

This story was begun in 1993 after reading "The Nine Nations of North America" by Joel Garreau. It was completed in 1997 and revised and e-published in 2000. The e-publisher went out of business shortly after that. It has been lightly revised again in 2006.

The reference to a fire in New Orleans in 2005 was written sometime in 1996 so was not corrected to 'hurricane' which would have fit reality. Still, it's pretty spooky.

References to Desksets and the Net have not been changed since they were originated in 1994. This can be evidenced by the form email addresses take with the inclusion of a server name in the domain extension. Maybe that's dated, or maybe that's just indicating we'll have to go back to requiring server identification in the future. Only Steve's Dad knows for sure.

ISBN: 978-0-6151-5790-0

"To my friends of the past who gave me inspiration for this.
To Eileen who is my future."

Acknowledgements:

This will never cover it all as the work took so long to come together. But I'll try. Thanks to NPR's library for exposing me to "The Nine Nations of North America." Terry Michael of the Washington Center for Politics and Journalism which gave me the internship in 1993 that afforded me the inspiration material. To Natalie Keith for looking at my first sketches of the map and not calling it totally crazy. To Misty Coffman for giving me the time and space to start writing and hearing my endless ideas. To the endless number of Austinites who allowed me to jabber on about the ideas in the book. Especially thanks to those Austinites who spent a few weeks reading through the radio broadcasts with the idea of making them into a radio play. To Mark Mauer, Nick Kanel, Mark Jurgena, Theresa Noyes, Tim Josserand, Pat Mcgill, Jeb Marlowe, Kevin Carney, Dan Gehrig, Chris Condry, and Sandy Marshall for leeting me steal inspiration from them. Special thanks to Cindi Harrison for above and beyond inspiration and editing. To Barb Matuzak for the idea to go first person. To the late and lamented CrossroadsPub.com for the first e-publication. To Regina Preciado for reading, encouraging and pointing out that Steve has dark hair. To Andy Melton and Kevin C. for re-insipring me to publish at Lulu.com. To Roger Chang for making remember I wrote it. And finally to Eileen Rivera for putting up with me and my crazy ideas. You rock.

THE PRESIDENT - 1
Washington, DC

The sunshine glowed hot and red through the office window. As it set, the President felt as if it might never rise again. He looked at the executive order on his desk. He knew the consequences.

The trouble in the Dakotas would escalate. Texas would try to bolt. The entire country would strain. It was all he could do. Some decades ago, there had been a surplus. It dried up as people lived longer and retired in droves. Not to mention the expense of pet projects of past Presidents. Now the country faced problems ten times worse than the money woes of the late 20th century.

He gazed out the window at the orderly green lawn, lit brightly in the mid-day. Not a soul stirred in that yard. 40 million people waited to hear what he would say tonight. None of them expected what would happen. None of them were prepared. He knew his country. All of history would come crashing down on their heads in the next few days and they would complain about the traffic.

Not until the stores emptied, or the TV went dark, would they really take notice. Then too late they would throw open the windows and find the world changed around them.

"Sleep well tonight," he said to no one but the sun. "Nothing will ever be the same again."

STEVE - 1
Austin, Texas

"For everything?" bellowed the woman standing over the pile of books she'd brought in to sell.

"Well, yes. We make an offer on everything you bring in. This stack here is what we can sell. If there's anything in this pile you want to hold on to it wouldn't really change the offer."

"You're trying to cheat me." The well-dressed but heavily made-up woman shook her head and jangled her gold-plated earrings.

"No ma'am. I assure you, I'm not trying to cheat--"

"This place is a rip off. Do you know how much these books cost me?"

"If you'd like to hold onto them that's fine but I'm afraid--"

"Just give me the $4," she snapped.

It was another in a series of forgettable moments in an arduous day. After the woman was at a safe distance, I made some cheap spurious remarks about her taste in clothing and then looked at the clock. It was six.

"I'm off Larry. I'll see you."

"Bye Steve." He was intent on another pile of books just brought in by an overweight man in a wheelchair.

Sweat exploded from my pores less than twenty seconds after I walked out the door. The heat of Austin, Texas settled on me like a drunk on a barstool. I got in my car and gingerly put my keys in the ignition, careful not to touch the searing hot steering column. I started the car, turned on the radio and blasted the A/C.

I hadn't listened to much radio since the latest budget crisis started. Helen was boycotting the news, so I did too. But curiosity finally got the better of me. A talk show host's animated voice barked out a monologue about the budget bill and the fate of the country, once again, hanging in the balance. The yammering ground to a halt and the American Belief Radio theme music carried in Greg Whitney, the deep-voiced slow-speaking ABR voice of reason. His tone and pitch always promised the truth. I wonder how his kids took it when he told them there was no Santa Claus.

"As Congress nears the deadline for the emergency economic plan, the President called for compromise. Republicans still call the social programs 'Johnson-like' and claim they will weaken the nation. Congressional Democrats accuse the Republicans of trying to destroy developing communities within the nation while sending the country into further depression. Speaker of the House Carmen Hinojosa made a fiery speech today from the floor calling for a last ditch compromise.

'We cannot continue to exhume the past while ignoring the needs of our many communities. This is not a Republican, Democratic or Libertarian issue.

We must come together for the good of the PEOPLE of America.'

"Meanwhile, the South Dakota National Guard still fights to keep order in Pierre, where Native American radicals demand reforms. Experts fear the situation may escalate into a battle for control of the city.

"And finally, the Texas Legislature approved a plan to bring the Texas National Guard under state control. Texas Governor Richard Morgan strongly denied this was a secessionary move:

'We feel to more flexibly respond to the rising tide of crime among the poor, an independent unit which does not need to mess with the federal bureaucracy every time it is needed, will be much more effective.'

"Critics call the separation unconstitutional and fear Texas will not use it for policing crime. I'm Greg Whitney for American Belief Radio."

"Thank you Greg. You're listening to ABR's America Considered. Let's hear now from ABR Washington commentator, Damian Mortley, with Eye on Washington."

KOLBRASKI - 1
Highland, Illinois

No one ever mentioned the middle of the country. The heartland. No one noticed and no one listened to us. For two years we knew of the Texas plans. Even now the country pretended not to see the signs.

I looked down into my coffee.

"You want anything else sir?"

I looked up into the beaming face of the waitress. Her bright expression dimmed considerably as I stared at her. The pain and despair of a hidden life and a terrible secret apparently showed more than I thought.

"No thanks."

"Uh... all right then... I'll just bring you the check."

I opened the manila folder and re-read the latest reconnaissance and planning documents. We needed a driver and I knew where to get one. But I didn't like my own idea one bit.

I paid and went back to the car. I could always get someone else but somehow I knew where it all led. A small part of me always felt a sense of destiny. My priest always tried to convince me it was "the call." Maybe it was. But not in the way he meant.

A fire burned in the distance. Smoke rose towards the heavens. It seemed to heat the whole sky. I started my car and watched the flames. That was my future.

STEVE - 2
Austin, Texas

I sat in the parking lot with the windows down to cool the car while the A/C began to work. Customers hurried through the lot to escape the heat into the cool bookstore. I lit a cigarette. One of my least favorite Netradio columnists began to exhort another of the multitude of perspectives on the crisis.

"People tighten their belts as the economic decline continues, while Congress works to beat the deadline to fund national services, like hospitals, toll roads, schools and police. The strangest thing to me, is the talk shows and the news analysts don't sound too worried. Oh, people hotly debate the merits of Gloria Presley's love escapades but they just laugh off Congress. 'What do you expect?' people say, 'Congress can't do anything right.' They treat the government like a bad sitcom. Tonight, Congress announces its economic plan. The talk shows are all analyzing how much the Republicans will be hurt by the inevitable compromise. All the pundits busily review who's who in the front row for the President's announcement. The fact that America goes bankrupt if there is no agreement has only briefly been touched on as something theoretically possible but inconceivable. 'Of course they'll compromise,' say the pundits,' and problems will be put off for yet another year as always.' I wonder. If people care that little, is the nation even worth saving? I only pray that my skepticism proves unfounded. I'm Damian Mortley with Eye on Washington."

As Mortley finished I looked up to find a beefy man in a gaudy orange shirt staring at me through the window.

"Damian Mortley huh?"

"Yeah."

"A bunch of fuckin' Liberal bullshit if you ask me. We need to throw everybody out, if you ask me."

"I didn't." I realized I was way too tired to get in an argument. My mouth didn't seem to care."You vote last election?"

"Oh well, I usually vote but I was on vacation."

"Uh-huh. Coulda voted early."

"Yeah but you know, spur of the moment shit like that throws off the best plans."

The man began to walk away.

"You have plenty of time to whine though don't you," I shouted after him.

The man flashed me a dirty look as I put the car in gear and moved out into Guadalupe Street rush hour traffic. I turned off the radio. After a day of inane questions and boredom, the heat turned my brain to sludge. I wanted to stop and eat at the Real Inn but I knew Helen was probably cooking. She'd get disappointed if I didn't come straight home. 27 years old and still on a leash.

The news wore on me. There was no pattern. I stretched my thin frame and yawned. What would happen if the shit really hit the fan? I looked down at my blue-collared work shirt, black jeans and wing-tips. Well dressed for Armageddon, I thought.

The light changed and I let the GPS drive from there to the 45th Access Point. We were all living a lie I decided none too profoundly, but it cheered me up somewhat because I couldn't handle what we were living as the truth. I wanted to rant. That's what everyone did. No action, just ranting. The Los Angeles Peace Party ranted about separatism, the Aryan Nation ranted about supremacy, the African-American Front ranted about racism, the Lakota Nation ranted about equality and the Texans ranted about independence from federal incompetence. Ranting made good TV and relieved everyone. Like cooling vents on a hot coil. The heat rises but the vent keeps everything stable... to a point. How far would it go before anger blew the vents and burst the coil?

The car rolled off the 45th Street Access Point and I took over, pulling into my parking lot. I thought of the 100 or so people in my apartment complex. All angry, I hoped, sitting at home ranting. The stairs were extremely steep as I climbed up to my apartment. The smell of Helen's famous pasta sauce drifted out to meet me and helped me up the last flight.

"Hey Steve," she squeaked as I walked in the door. "You look beat."

I trudged in putting on my best 1950's accountant act.

"Tough day at the office?" she asked, humoring me.

I threw my lanky body down on the couch. "It's dog eat dog out there honey. A man's gotta strive, gotta push or they'll eat ya alive." I jumped back up to follow her. "Whatcha cookin'? Can I help?" I was looking over her shoulder at the bubbling red things and the steaming onions.

"No, but you could set up the machine to record Daystrom because I know you'll want to watch that stupid press conference."

"Ok." I backed away from the sautéing onions before I started to cry. "I'll probably just listen to it in the bedroom on radio. I dig hearing the news on radio. Makes it seem more like news that way. Like people listening to war reports in the 1940's."

"I can't believe you keep that old thing around when we have a perfectly good Deskset."

"Helen, my radio is different. It's nostalgic. Like time travel."

"How can you have nostalgia for a time you never lived in?"

"I don't know. It just seems like people were more of a unit then. Everyone, even the low class and poor, kind of went in the same general direction. Now everyone's all over the place. Things move too fast, too decentralized. Everything's falling apart."

"Oh hush."

She stirred the sauce with a wooden spoon. She wore simple black jeans and a plain purple shirt. Her auburn hair just touched her shoulders in a straight bob. Thick framed glasses covered her mild blue eyes. A simple ensemble, straightforward, practical and tasteful, just like her. In this light she was attractive, pretty, but not beautiful.

Picking up two plates heaped with steaming pasta, she waltzed over to the couch and sat down next to me. As usual she brought water for her but I had to get up and get my own.

We ate and talked, avoiding the news. It made Helen unhappy to think about it and so she just refused. I never have understood her almost paranoid fear of the world at large. She sometimes screamed and left the room after two minutes of news.

"I just hate hearing and seeing all that stuff. There's nothing I can do about it, so why should I worry," she would say when pressed.

We ate and played a round of Whist. Then Helen sat up on the couch to watch Daystrom. "You go brave the ugliness, and then give me the highlights."

She shooed me away.

I curled up on the bed and tuned in one of the few stations left that simulcast on the net and regular air. Most of these stations were National Public Radio or its federally supported commercial competition, American Belief Radio. I preferred ABR because it seemed more real and more old-time. NPR had a stiff snooty air about it.

GOVERNOR MORGAN - 1
Austin, Texas

Across town in the Governor's mansion, Richard Morgan enjoyed the same radio broadcast as Steve, for many of the same reasons. Morgan had an old fashioned streak and enjoyed the drama of radio. It gave the occasion importance. The broadcast began.

"It's 9:00 at KLBJ Austin," a local voice toned in over the news theme.

"This is American Belief Radio News, I'm Greg Whitney. The President will deliver a nationwide media address in just a few minutes. We'll bring that to you live but first a summary of today's other top stories.

"The group 'Lakota Nation' reinforced its midnight deadline for Native American autonomy in the Dakotas by surrounding all state buildings with armed men, including the two state capitol buildings. Police and National Guard troops stood watch to prevent disturbances but remained inactive. The bankrupt South Dakota legislature has not paid the police force in over a month. Guard troops will wait until the President's announcement, before attempting to disperse the Lakota Nation militants.

"Texas Governor Richard Morgan threatened to do, quote, 'whatever is necessary' to protect Texas' interests if Congress fails to pass a satisfactory economic package. Texas put its National Guard troops under state control today. Many fear Texas might try to secede before the Supreme Court rules on the removal. Officials on both sides of the issue call these fears alarmist.

"And now, we take you to the White House for the President's address:"

Morgan fumbled with a pencil as he waited for the address to begin. He knew what was coming. The damned federalists wouldn't listen to him. They had finally pushed things too far. If the President's address went as expected there was only one God-given course Morgan could take to protect the families of honest people given into his care.

The pencil broke.

He leaned in toward his radio. His gnarled features glowed blood red in the light of the dial. Deep crevices of black lined his face where years of maneuvering and deal-cutting had left their mark. His cold blue eyes burned with anticipation. His face grew angry at the idea of what the

President would say but deep inside his glacial soul he wanted this excuse more than anything in the world. It wasn't for freedom, it wasn't for Texas, it was for Richard Morgan. He wanted the chance to realize what he knew he had been born to do. Take the reigns, any reigns, and lead a people to a higher, better state.

A gavel sounded, and a voice broke through. "Ladies and Gentlemen, the President of the United States of America." Staged applause erupted through the speakers.

A man with a slightly southern accent began to intone in the methodical pattern that had swept him into office.

"Good evening fellow Americans. I called this address tonight with the hopes of bringing you the good news of an economic compromise that could work for all. Unfortunately, the political gridlock of partisanship has prevented that compromise from being reached and tomorrow the nation goes bankrupt. I have, regretfully and with trepidation, prepared an executive plan that I hoped I would not have to use. But I will... because this nation is too great and too proud to sink into the embarrassment of bankruptcy."

Morgan's eyes glowed and spun with raging delight. Back across town and slightly uphill, Steve's heart sank at what he guessed would follow.

"Therefore, effective at noon tomorrow, I will sign executive orders declaring martial law in many parts of the nation where police forces go unfunded. All remaining money will be transferred, on emergency status, to the military, which will fill the positions left empty by Congress. Those left unemployed by the federal government will have assistance and several corporations have agreed to provide easy hiring to former federal employees. Eventually we hope to hire you back. The executive orders will limit the military to performing civilian roles under civilian law. Each order will be effective for only one month at a time, to allow us to re-evaluate what is needed each month. This will not be a dictatorship. These orders will remain well within constitutional limits. If Congress can pass a plan which will put the federal government back on its feet, then these orders will be countermanded immediately.

"I thank you for your patience and assistance and I know together... as Americans... the nation can pull through the tough times ahead. Let us not forget the words of our greatest president, Abraham Lincoln; 'United We Stand, Divided We Fall.' Thank you, God Bless You and God Bless America."

"This is American Belief Radio."

"The New Saturn Kennedys are Heeeeeeeeeeeeeeeere. And the financing is better than ever before...."

STEVE - 3
Austin, Texas

I turned down the sounded and waited for the analysis from ABR's team of marginally intelligent political pundits.

"This is American Belief Radio, I'm Greg Whitney. With me are Elizabeth Rochester, Professor of Political Science at the University of Michigan, Ellen Mubarique, Chief Analyst of America First's political division and JoseLuis Pena, former Secretary of Commerce under President Jane Michael."

The analysts cut the speech into its constituent signs, symbols and signifiers. They fawned over the signals sent out to Texas and South Dakota and the powerful use of Abraham Lincoln, even though Lincoln didn't actually say the 'united we stand' quote. I noticed they ignored the fascist aspects of the orders and the fact that a president who was denying that the country was in danger of civil war, was using the ghost of Lincoln to bolster his position.

I knew why too. If the President let the country slip into bankruptcy, the government would have to submit to UN stewardship of the economy until the nation was solvent. That was certainly better than martial law, where constitutional freedoms became questionable. But neither party wished to test the irrational fear of the UN that had bred itself in the more suspicious citizens of the US. The analysts finished by agreeing that this was as bad as it could possibly get.

I walked quietly into the front room and found Helen on the phone, her face blank.

"Yeah, I uh--understand... ok. Well it's certainly not your fault Mindy... yes I know. Well," she sighed, "I guess that's what I'll do then. All right. See you later."

"Mindy?"

"Yeah. She called to tell me not to come to work tomorrow because all non-military related jobs have been temporarily laid off. That means the library will operate with a skeleton crew of the most senior and most Texan staff. Fuck it, I was born in Lubbock. I don't see why years of state residency should have anything to do with why you're kept on or not!"

"What about job servicing?"

"Well, she said there'd be some sort of federal--corporate job bank but the University of Texas isn't involved, so of course they won't tell anybody anything about it."

"That's not exactly what I'd call easy hiring."

"What?" Helen looked annoyed.

"The President promised easy hiring and that's exactly what you're not getting."

"I don't know. I guess I'll just go to the unemployment office tomorrow and see what's up there."

"You and 200,000 of your closest friends."

"Will you shut up." Helen looked away. "It's hard enough without being negative."

"I'm sorry, I was just... pointing out the facts that's all. I mean, you have to face them..."

"Well, why do you have to be the one in charge of making me face them?" she yelled, "You face them. Leave me alone. Why does this all have to happen now? Why to us? Why?" She looked at me plaintively now, as if I somehow knew the answer and could make everything better.

But I couldn't. I didn't know what to do to stop it either and worse, I didn't care. I felt like slapping her for some reason and telling her to get over it and get on with her life. Complaining and whining won't make it better. Instead, I said softly, "Come here."

She stepped toward me and I held her tight, staring into the corner waiting for the right amount of time to pass.

"It's going to be ok, " I spat out quickly while my face grew hot with anger. Why couldn't she be stronger? We agreed to forget it for the moment and headed off to bed.

I lay beside her quietly wishing she wasn't there. I feared she could hear my thoughts, or somehow divine them by my movements and my breathing. I feared her. That's why she angered me. I feared getting close, feeling responsible, and having to help her. I didn't want the responsibility of soothing her insecurities when I had so many of my own.

I needed her strength to bolster mine and I felt she sucked mine away. Every minute I devoted to calming her, or helping her, depleted my reserve of self-sufficiency. I felt that reserve nearing empty.

As I drifted off to sleep, I imagined her limping along a dusty road. I walked beside her trying to keep her from falling. She told me how to turn and what to do to keep her up.The longer we walked the closer to the ground I came. As I fell to sleep I met the ground and felt her standing straight and upright on top of me as I buried my face in the dirt.

KOLBRASKI - 2
Greenville, Illinois

I sat at the poker table eying my two buddies, John and Gehrig. I knew they were steamed at this last hand and I was lapping it up.

"Sorry boys. Couldn't help it."

"Fuck, Kolbraski. Let me see your sleeves."

"Shut up John, I've got short sleeves." I flapped them open for everyone to see.

"That supposed to convince me of anything?"

Gehrig went and sat in the corner to smoke. He knew I didn't approve of his habit so he always got as far away from me as possible. I just wanted to help.

"Hell of a thing that announcement," Gehrig said to nobody.

John rose from the couch, annoyed. "Shit. Why'd you have to bring that up Gehrig."

"I don't know that it's such a BAD thing necessarily. Maybe it's what we need to get back on our feet."

"Or destroy the country," I shot back.

"What's left of it," added John.

"Why are you two always so down on the nation. We're still the second largest power in the world. We're third in food production. We even have one of the top military forces."

I shared a glance with John. "Listen to your numbers Gehrig. No firsts. And yet, the government just keeps on goin' as if nothin' is wrong. Shit man, I'm not a big UN fan but I'd almost rather see us hook into one of those economic stupidship things than live under federal martial law."

"Yeah, well, what are you gonna do about it Kolbraski. Go to your Psych Association Meetings and whine about Cortex research?" needled Gehrig.

A sly smile crept across my face like a bug.

John laughed. "Yeah, Gehrig that's exactly what he's going to do."

"Shut up John." We didn't need to lead Gehrig that way. Not yet.

"I didn't say nothing," John muttered as he took another Coke out of the refrigerator.

Gehrig stood up. "Well Kolby, you wanna ride in together tomorrow?"

"Yeah I'll meet you at McDonald's at eight."

"Sounds good. See ya John."

"Bye Gehrig."

I waited for the door to close and turned on John. "Can't you keep your big mouth shut. He gets more suspicious all the time."

"Why don't you just invite him in?" John stared directly at me.

"Because. I don't want to take that responsibility. You joined all on your own, without me. You remember how much we talked about whether we should both be in this thing? I think it should be like that for everybody."

John shook his head. "We all heard from someone, Kolby. It might as well be from you. Besides, with you and me it's a bit different."

"I guess. But I just can't drag Gehrig in. I can't. Not unless things really get hairy. I'm gonna hit the sack. G'night."

"Night." John picked up a copy of 'Protector' magazine. "I'll be in, in a while."

From my bedroom window, I saw Gehrig leaning against a post on the front porch of our house. I knew he didn't like to smoke in his car. At least that would've been his excuse if I nabbed him eavesdropping.

I could tell he didn't know what to do with the information he'd just heard. I also knew he was quick enough to figure it out before long. He walked down the steps and got into his two year old brown Saturn Guthrie and drove off.

I leaned back on my bed and turned on the box. They blabbed on about the President's speech, the Texas Army and the Lakota Nation. It all seemed unreal to me, living in Greenville. Nothing ever changed here. A business closed or opened occasionally. Rumors started about some big building scheme on the edge of town which would ruin the already dead downtown area. What would happen if Texas seceded? If the Lakota Nation rioted in Pierre? Nothing would happen to Greenville. You'd still have to drive twenty miles to get to a decent department store. There wasn't much chance of any history happening. That's why people were so paranoid and useless at the same time. They kept hearing about bad things happening around the country but they never happened to them, so they got paranoid waiting for the axe to fall. Some got soft over the years noticing that whichever way they voted for President, nothing seemed to change in their immediate locale. I didn't want that to happen to me. I wanted to be there and know, man. I wanted to know.

The Sun - 1

The night wore out giving way to sunrise. The summer sun rolled through one more day as Helen hunted jobs and Steve hunted reasons. The sun beat through the office window of Texas Governor Richard Morgan as he eyed the bill that could likely become a piece of history. His allies in Congress had drafted the Secession Resolution on his request. He held the fate of Texas and perhaps the US in his hands. He could still back out and he would, if he weren't sure this was the only way to maximize the benefits.

He held it up to the light, a piece of history. His to make or not make, gleaming black on white, waiting for his gesture to send it into motion. A man making history with the sun beating on him, warming him, making him feel the rush of the moment flood through him and exhilarate him. In his mind, he imagined himself sharing a timeless experience with Caesar, Napoleon, even Hitler. He pressed the intercom button ceremoniously.

The sun moved on, scorching New Mexico and Oklahoma, where the military patrolled small town streets and the court system welcomed its first MPs as bailiffs. It streaked up the mountains of Colorado, shining on a woman biking up a hill in Denver.

FAYE & JEFF - 1
Denver, Colorado

Faye rolled up to my house and carried her bike up the porch. She had tied her blonde hair in a bun and wore granny glasses, a white T-shirt and jeans. She knocked over a stack of old Denver Posts as she went in the door.

"Hellooo! I've come to rob the house. Give me all your money now."

I jumped out from my hiding place behind the door, blasting away with a potato gun.

"God, you idiot!" Faye laughed. "What's your problem."

I tried to jump past her to get another round off. She pulled me down on the couch and we kissed.

"How's life on the farm?" I asked.

"We found two very nice kittens, two very nice homes today, thank you."

 "You're so dedicated."

"I know. What do you want to do about dinner?"

"Well, I thought about ordering pizza."

"I wanted to go out to eat." She was so cute when she whined.

"I can't. I'm waiting for a phone call, you know, from Professor Croslin. It's about that photo grant."

I had put in an application for a grant to shoot indigenous people in the Black Hills of the Dakotas. There was a lot going on there with the Lakota Nation activists and I thought I had a pretty good chance at the grant. Geez, I mean, who could turn down politics, native Americans and natural beauty all wrapped up in one beautiful little funded package.

"Well fine, be that way." Faye picked up the phone and smirked. "Shall I cook... or you?" She teased me but she knew how much I wanted this grant.

"You cook. I'll handle the ambiance."

I turned on the Deskset and looked for some music to play. Although Faye wasn't into slick rock as much as I was, we both liked The Couldabeens, a New Orleans band with a small following in Denver. I searched around but for some reason couldn't find their album PunkRoseTart. The Deskset played a Nouveau Lounge group from Boston, covering 'Mas Que Nada' and it interfered with my concentration. Nouveau Lounge makes me want to start heaving bowling balls through plate glass windows. Suddenly, the music stopped and I snapped my head up as an unfamiliar shrill tone screamed from the speakers.

(Beeeeeeeeeeeeeeeeeeeeeeeeeeeeeeeeeeeeeeep)

"Ladies and Gentlemen your attention please. A red alert state of national emergency has been declared for the states of North and South Dakota, more information to follow."

"This is not a test. This is not a test. Citizens in the States of North Dakota and South Dakota are advised to seek shelter and stay indoors. Assistance is on the way from the United States Army. Do not take part in the fighting. Defend yourself only in extreme necessity. Do not take up arms and enter the conflict. Repeat. Citizens of North Dakota and South Dakota are advised to seek shelter and stay indoors. Assistance is on the way from the United States Army. Do not take part in the fighting. Defend yourself only in extreme necessity. Do not take up arms and enter the conflict."

(Beeeeeeeeeeeeeeeeeeeeeeeeeeeeeeeeeeeeeeep)

"The previous was not a test. This was a national emergency broadcast system alert. If you did not hear all the instructions, you are advised to call 511 immediately. Once again if you did not hear the emergency broadcast system instructions, call 511 immediately."

The broadcast fell silent for a few seconds. Faye absentmindedly hung up the phone. She had stopped talking to the pizza place halfway through the announcement.

"This is the American Belief Radio Network in New York. Details are still sketchy out of the Dakotas but it appears Pierre and Bismarck, the capitals of South and North Dakota respectively, have come under attack from the extremist Lakota Nation militia. While the emergency warning covered the Dakotas as a whole, however, no action is reported outside the capitals--uhhh, correction... weee're also getting reports of fighting in Aberdeen and Rapid City and US-83, the North South road between the two capitals has reportedly been commandeered by the Lakota Nation. We're also getting unconfirmed reports that other groups from other areas of the Dakotas have joined the fighting and according to this--report--they have occupied the center of North Dakota and most of the western half of South Dakota already. Uh--Uh--Apparently this action has been planned for some time and the occupied territories are orderly and proceeding with everyday business. That from BBC correspondent Rex Hamburg on the Cheyenne River Reservation.

"American Belief Radio will keep you informed as soon as more information becomes available."

Timpani drums began beating and a Darth Vader voice boomed out, "UPRISING IN THE DAKOTAS--An ABR Special Report."

"I guess the photo trip to the Black Hills is off." I couldn't hide my disappointment. Faye turned with a friendly glare.

"Shhhh."

"American Belief Radio now joins Lakota Nation leader John Blacknight from Pierre, South Dakota."

An atonal and somewhat timid voice came over the speakers, "...if you'll just bear with us a moment. (eeeewwee) Ok, Mr. Blacknight will now make a brief statement to the press and answer a few questions." A tumult of voices, clunks, clicks and scraping chairs filled the gap.

They receded under the presence of an articulate, measured and deadly serious voice.

"Thank you General Johnson. I would like to tell the US people what is going on here. All of North Dakota from the Montana border to Interstate 29 has been secured including Grand Forks. The front stretches from Watertown to Mitchell, south to Yankton. The Lakota Nation has been realized. Our capital is in Oglala, the symbolic site of our long struggle for freedom. Let me say now also, that we were quite willing to work within the framework of the US constitution, as a sovereign state of the union, until that constitution was thrown on the dung heap. The white man has broken his last treaty, a treaty with himself. We are a friendly open nation and invite the community of nations to open negotiations with us. We declare our enemies to be the army of the USA, and any nation which provides direct military assistance to that army. We are not against the allies of the US, or the people of the US, if they are not against us."

A burst of noise followed, cut short by the nasal voice of an eastern reporter.

"Mr. Blacknight do you really believe your 'nation' could survive independently, not only militarily but economically?"

"We are a proud and productive people and already have trade pacts signed to go into effect."

Reporters began shouting Mr. Blacknight's name until one shouted the others down.

"When you say you have secured territory does that really mean everyone in the territory you claim supports your actions?"

"Secured territories either have the willing allegiance of the people or have ceased resisting and are negotiating local autonomy. We will welcome all non-Native Americans if they are willing to support the Lakota Nation. We will also have a reservation for those wishing to be separate and we offer safe passage out of the country for those who wish to leave. Those are all the questions I can take right now. Thank you."

The broadcast returned to Greg Whitney.

"American Belief Radio now joins a press conference in progress from Washington, Columbia where the President and the Joint Chiefs of Staff are commenting on the Dakota riots."

A voice with little expression, except for a tinge of a Brooklyn accent, droned on in the middle of an apparently long answer to a reporter's question.

"...very much exaggerated. They have seized certain government and communication buildings but their activities are limited to the larger cities in the Dakotas and we have them on the run in all but the capitals, where they are holed up in state buildings. Once again, do not believe their claims. Do not believe their boasts. They have no government, they have no support and they have no chance but to surrender to the US Army and restore order. We beseech them to avoid needless bloodshed in this ill-fated enterprise. Thank you."

The noise of the press conference ended abruptly and Greg Whitney spoke into the silence.

"The voice of General Cameron Abdullah, the Chairman of the Joint Chiefs of Staff.

"So the Lakota Nation declaring they have won control of the Dakotas, reporting 20 dead and 300 wounded Lakota as well as an estimated 60 US Guardsmen dead and 400 wounded. The Joint Chiefs of Staff reporting that the Lakota do NOT have control and casualties are limited. ABR will keep you updated as the situation becomes clearer.

"In another late-breaking development, the State of Texas has declared a state-wide emergency due to looting in several smaller towns not yet covered by martial law. Texas deployed its Texas Army National Guard to help restore order. This has been an American Belief Radio special report."

The station rather unfortunately returned to lounge music, leaving Faye and me gaping at each other.

"I don't... believe it... really." Faye could barely speak.

"My project better damn well still be on. This could be the most important story of the decade, you know."

"Who knows whether it will be on or not, Jeff. I mean, they might not let you in no matter who or why or where."

"Don't be negative. I mean--" The phone rang and I stopped talking to get it. Faye listened to me spit out a mess of yeses and O ks. The phone call ended before I realized what had taken place.

"Was that professor Croslin?"

"Oh, yeah. He said the project is still on as long as the Lakota Nation agrees, WHICH," I tried to stop a knowing look from developing on Faye's face, "he says is very likely from what he knows about the group. You know, he has some friends at SDU who are close with a few of the Lakota Nation's big shots."

"So I can come too, right?" Faye chirped, kidding and hopeful at the same time.

"Of course. I'll need security in a developing country like that."

Faye laughed. "You'll get more than security, ya big palooka."

"I'm serious. I'm going to try to talk them into letting you go. You think you can get off work? You're a great help and I'll need it."

"Well, yeah. I mean if they'll really let me, sure." Faye looked at me stunned. She got the look on her face that meant she was trying to figure out how much of what I was saying was crap. "No problem. Kim's a doll. She'd let me off work for having a hang-nail."

"But... We'll be unchaperoned. Won't that be dangerous?"

"Oh dear. Well, let me show you the dangers."

The Sun - 2

The burning sun moved through the sky over California. Unceasing in its slow circle, it crossed the ocean through the integrated economies of Asia, into the vital markets of Europe and once again reached the empty budget of the USA.

The United States of a crumbling America, brewing hot as the sun under the President's emergency plan. The flames of discontent heated the great melting pot. The nation swayed and swelled in the heat. Someone needed to cool things off before the pot boiled over and destroyed itself. But Congress would not move to douse the flame.

The United States stood alone outside the UN driven economic programs of the other continents. Infrequent UN failures were touted in the US as proof that sovereignty and freedom always prevailed. Supporters of the UN plans argued that an integrated world economy was not inconsistent with sovereignty and freedom.

The sun ignored these economic problems. Unaffected by the political heat, it crept into the Midwest. US Army Patrolmen gazed up at the hot July morning, moving along Midwestern streets, looking for suspicious citizens. The Army detained even potential looters by order of the President. The freedom of righteous US citizens must be protected.

A thin edge of sunlight seared the Mississippi River and wound through the piny woods of Louisiana and East Texas. It arrived in the Texas hill country and beat through Steve's bedroom window.

STEVE - 4
Austin, Texas

I was dreaming about sand.

I sat on a white picket fence in the middle of a desert watching a toad slowly die. In the distance, I could hear rumbling that reminded me of beans cooking on the stove. In the air, I smelled burnt motor oil and grease. Helen lay in the sand covering her ears. The fence seemed extremely high. I tried to get Helen to help me down but she kept screaming as the rumbling got louder. Finally the sand began to buckle and Helen sunk down into it. I dove off the fence into the sand to save her but the sand had turned into hot water. I found myself lying on a broken piece of asphalt floating in a hot sea. I called for Helen but she didn't answer. I grew weary of calling and lay down on the asphalt, hot and sweating with a light breeze blowing across my feet.

I woke up sweating under the covers my feet sticking out form under them. Goddamn. I squinted at the window and closed the blinds. In the kitchen Helen had left out a croissant. I washed it down with a glass of water and headed to work. We argued this morning about something before I fell back to sleep, like I always did, after she left for work. I tried to remember what it was about but couldn't.

The Hyde Park neighborhood was bright and sunny. Folks in the old Victorian mansions that littered the area puttered around in their gardens. Kids rode bicycles and joggers eyed cars warily. They'd better. If the doctors ever found out about my fantasies involving my car and joggers, I'd be put on medication quick. More serious bikers with backpacks and helmets, whom I respected, raced in and out of the traffic that clogged 45th Street. Why the city hadn't improved the transportation system in the last fifty years was beyond me. Cars only outnumbered bikes 3 to 1. It was dangerous for everyone, especially since people in Austin did not know how to drive.

I finally got the nerve to pull out of the parking lot into a brief gap in the morning stream of vehicles.

I thought about my friend Kolbraski back in Southern Illinois. Sunny days always reminded me of pitching baseballs to Kolby back in the summer after High School. A Minnesota Twins baseball scout had called and for two weeks, I'd tried to help him prepare. Nothing had come of his baseball career but it had got him into college where he excelled as a student leader. I forgave him for the leader part and respected his mind. He was always a bit more of an organization man than me but seemed to hold on to his identity very well.

I'd called him yesterday just to see how he was doing. He sounded real suspicious of the Texan secession bill but more than that, he just sounded suspicious. I noticed it particularly when he talked about the Psychological Association meetings he attended and apparently now chaired.

"I wish you could come to them. They're informative. Make me feel safer. We could use you... at the meetings I mean. Your ideas and stuff."

"What do you mean you could use me? I live 1,000 miles away. In Texas."

"Well... I don't know. It's just always great to have creative minds, man."

He sounded suspiciously oblique.

"Sounds like you want to experiment on me."

"Not hardly. Forget about the Psych Association, did you see the Blues got sold back to Ralston-Purina..."

Kolbraski changed the subject but I still wondered what the Psych Association was all about. Fucked up drug stuff? It had happened to cleaner-cut friends of mine. Internet Pirates? A lucrative and dangerous game that would appeal to Kolbraski's intellect and sense of excitement. Covert militias? They were around more than ever and recruited people just like Kolbraski.

I passed a truck of men in green and looked for my old roommate Ray who was in the National Guard. I wondered how Ray was dealing with the Guard's detachment. Some Guardsmen had requested transfers to other states. I'd tried to call Ray yesterday but hadn't been able to get through.

I was so shaken by Kolbraski that I had decided to call my Dad. My Dad was 72 and acted 100. He had retired from SLIUS, the St. Louis Institute of Unified Studies, only five years before. His claim to fame was pioneering a new computer protocol which helped make the revolutionary Deskset possible. The Deskset replaced the old personal computer in little over a year after the protocol was tested. It combined all possible forms of communication, intelligence and computation into one large network of light, portable units. Instead of having smaller computers linked by phone lines to larger computers, the Deskset turned the entire Internet into one large computer. It operated like a cell, acting independently while drawing on the computational power of every other Deskset hooked up to the net.

The large computer companies had almost crushed it, because it eliminated the need for costly hard drives and processors. It also greatly hindered eavesdropping and mail tapping because the system worked non-linearly. If one sent a narrow enough message only the recipient's retina could withdraw it. Anyway, my Dad had not become rich having only been a member of the Deskset team and an academic to boot. "It's like being the world's leading expert on evaporated milk," he had said once.

Yesterday, he was a bit crotchety when I called him.

"When are you gettin' the hell out of Texas. Man, I wouldn't stay there a day longer if they paid me."

"I told you, Dad, we're working on it. I do think it's best that we leave. Helen can't find a job anyway."

"How is Helen. Still quiet?"

My Dad always managed to say something that totally baffled me. I replied, "Sure, I guess. She's fine except she can't find work and stuff."

"Just get up and go now, man. The whole mess is goin' down the tubes. You wait and see. Means of production finally ate out the raw middle. That's what I say. You ever listen to that Damian Mortley on the Net. He's almost a smart feller for bein' in Washington. Damned moderates."

"Look Dad, this is serious down here. They're gonna bolt. I just know it. There are people with somethin' to gain from it."

"You watch out for them Steve. They'll talk sweet to ya from day one. Unassuming types. The jerks aren't the ones to watch out for. They don't get any real power very often. But when they do.... You watch the mild ones and watch 'em close. They should be the first ones against the wall. Hitler was real quiet."

I laughed out loud to myself as I approached the store. I always loved talking to Dad. He was "a hoot" to use one of his own antiquated expressions.

Across the street from the bookstore, six soldiers were escorting a young man with long blonde hair into a truck. Perhaps the kid had been causing trouble. There WAS a lot of looting in the poor sections of town but Hyde Park wasn't poor. The idea of the army rounding up non-mainstream people made me shudder.

It took my eyes a few minutes to adjust to the dim store interior after the white-hot light outside. A few customers poked around the New

Arrivals section looking for something to help them ignore the growing trouble. Larry stood at the counter explaining to a man in a silk shirt that he had to be a teacher to receive a teacher's discount. American Belief Radio chattered out of the speakers.

A caller with a rural Midwestern accent spoke to the star ABR call-in host Jack Deleo.

"I just don't see why we don't just bomb em. We don't got no use for those states anyway. Those people are un-American and if they don't want to be part of our great nation they should leave or face the consequences."

Jack's mildly deep voice broke in, "What about the innocent people in the Dakotas sir? I don't think we can really just massively bomb and kill patriotic Americans. Don't you think we can rely on the US Army to solve this without wasting lives?"

"I don't know sir. I really don't know. I see your point but I think this government has got to do something drastic to solve its problems. I'm sick and tired of watching everyone sitting around on their butts."

"Sick and tired enough to secede or revolt?"

Silence.

The caller sounded unsure now.

"No... not exactly. But that's not the point." He began to pick up steam, "It's these terrorists that gotta be stopped. They don't even care about the nation," he finished sounding almost convinced.

Jack cut him off, "Well thank you sir, and I know you're not alone with a lot of those sentiments. We're going to break for news now with Jerry Martinez. This is American Belief Radio."

I walked off to the back in disgust. None of it seemed real. The military rule, the secession bill, the yahoos chanting for destruction. None of it. It wasn't happening. And yet somewhere, I knew, somebody was in jail for no reason. Right here in this country. My Dad was right. We had to get out of here. I walked through the buy-back area, past my co-workers who were busy at the counter buying rotten used books for no money. I went to the phone in the warehouse and called up my friend Mulu in Denton to talk about getting out.

"Hey Mulu what's up?"

"Nothing Steve. How've you been?"

"Wanting to come up to see you."

"I see....Be stayin' long?"

"NO... can't. Gotta keep movin', keep workin'. You know."

"Yeah, I know exactly what you're talkin' about. Hey, why don't I give you a call tonight? I'll have more time to talk and we can get together a plan."

"Sounds great."

"Ok, talk to you then."

"Cool. Bye."

I knew that when Mulu called me back that night, we would be able to talk freely. Mulu was highly adept at avoiding most all computer generated wiretaps.

Newcity of Chicago - 1

The city of Chicago had fallen far since the height of Mayor Daley's proud reign. Or had it? There were gangsters before Daley and gangs afterward. There were poor sections before Daley too, he just stacked them on top of each other in the world infamous Taylor homes. Traffic wasn't his fault. Not really. He hadn't invented the car had he? One thing Mayor Daley had instilled in Chicago was a sense of community. Even though he wholly misunderstood the black community and bordered on racism, he tried to unify the city as Chicagoans--sometimes to the point of xenophobia. That sense of community had wavered and faltered over the years, especially as the wealthy fled to the suburbs.

When the African-American Front formed, most saw it as another in a long line of militant black activist groups much like the Nation of Islam or the Black Panthers. What made the AAF different was its emphasis on community. Not black community, specifically, but the non-rich community. "Let the rich hide in their penthouses while we come hand to hand to knock their buildings down," read one AAF pamphlet. Championing the poor and redressing wrongs done to the black community were the AAF's two pillars. They promised to ride the rich, of any color, out of town on a rail and put African-Americans in charge for real.

Inspired by the success of the Lakota revolt, the AAF had sprung into action in several rust belt cities. Only in Chicago, Detroit and Philadelphia had there been much success yet. But in Chicago and Detroit, the success was overwhelming. Mayor Daley IV had already fled the city for Springfield. The City Police either defected or helped people evacuate, making the AAF job easier. Resistance was infrequent, actual gunfights rare.

The first thing the AAF did after the city was secured was a hasty remodel of O'Hare airport. Mayor Jamaal had made a point of keeping all train and air routes open through Chicago. In one short week, the structure was rebuilt with organized exits and entrances. The AAF guard ensured a smooth running airport. You followed the guard from gate to gate or you missed your flight and risked landing in jail. Not a light consideration in the Newcity which, although operating its major transit centers freely, was highly suspicious of 'foreigners.' Pushy people got nothing in the Newcity except maybe shot.

The AAF mostly wanted people's money. O'Hare was the only part of the Newcity most people would ever see. It became the easiest airport in North America in which to change planes. In addition to added revenue, Jamaal's transit policy insured his small country became indispensable to the rest of the world. The Newcity of Chicago operated a gate that enabled people to get away from trouble or into it, swiftly and efficiently.

The Sun - 3

The Sun sank slowly over the Texas hill country, shooting its rays at a sleek black car. The radiant silence of the setting was broken by the unmistakable cadence of Damian Mortley.

"What bothers me most about the latest events, is the callers on talk shows. Even with the nation in severe distress, the Cro-Magnon attitude hasn't changed. Bomb 'em all to hell, even if we kill our own. No one has any rights but us, even if they are us. But you know, nobody trusts the government any farther than they can throw them. One of these days we've got to make a choice. You either trust the communities, or you trust the nation. Apparently, we can't have it both ways and right now we have it neither way.

"And what is it with martial law? How long is this comedy playing? I can't buy an apple without being frisked. None of these hot rod callers criticizes Congress for failing to reach a plan. They just cynically remark on the gridlock that still prevents a compromise. You know, as the nation proves itself less and less trustworthy, folks are going to start shaking loose. Things like the Texas motion to secede will only gain support as long as martial law drags on. I'm Damian Mortley with 'Eye On Washington'."

As if pointing out something important, the Sun reached through the window of the sleek black car and illuminated Governor Morgan in an unnatural glow. The sun's extraordinary beam felt like a spotlight to the wizened man of 73. He looked in the mirror at his taut West Texas features. He thought he could see aged, timeless wisdom in the crevices of his face now sharp in the twilight. He always wore dark suits with starched white shirts and a blood red tie. He felt this accentuated his features best. Besides, the outfit made him feel like a minister of truth, rather than a politician. A hand like a mummy reached out and turned off the radio. He tilted his head back slightly, tightened his eyes and soaked in the view.

'Street lights and porch lamps dot the hills like the eyes of a hundred cats,' he thought. 'They're all watching to see what happens. They want to know what I know. Given to me to know, like a gift from above.'

The sun gave up in its attempt to point out the man and gave over the sky to night.

A dark black Volvo pulled up next to Morgan.

HANK - 1
Austin, Texas

I rolled down my windows as I approached Morgan's Mercedes. He looked out at me with his severe expression, which meant he'd been thinking about himself too much. Aside from being a member of the opposition party, Morgan scared me because of his penchant to babble about himself and Texas as if one and the same entity.

"Hello Hank." His voice crackled like the West Texas ground he grew up on.

"Rich." I nodded. I rarely called him Governor, not only because I didn't want to feed his fire but also because we had been junior senators together and had formed a friendly opposition. Hell, Rich Morgan had ensnared, by personality alone, the entire Texas Senate, House, and janitorial staff from the moment he stepped through the capitol doors. He had that strange political talent of changing your mind as you spoke, without him even saying a word or making a gesture.

We let the silence fill up. I finally gave up the waiting game.

"What's the story Rich?"

"Well... see, the Theocrats in my party want a prayer bill." He fidgeted a bit. "Hell's bells, they're crazy Hank, but it's not much and I believe we can hold them right there if we give it to 'em."

"Not Public Prayer." I cocked my head back and looked at him apprehensively.

"Uh, yeah, that's the one. No big deal. It's not like it's compulsory or nuttin.' People don't have to do it."

"But you know we're dead set against it. Can't have it, in fact." I tried to speak plainly. I didn't like the direction of this meeting already. I still wasn't sure why I'd agreed to it. Damned odd.

"Right, well, uh--course my moderates don't want it either. We can stomp it altogether, I think, but we're gonna need help..."

"On S.R. 8713. That's a tall order Rich."

"Right. 8713. That's the one... and I've, been think--well, that don't have nuttin' to do with this." His quick change of tone signaled a warning to me.

"What?"

"Nah, nah, it wouldn't be right. Could be seen as unethical. Just occurred to me is all." He shook his head to brush away the words he'd just said. They fell right in my lap, as I have no doubt he planned.

Emphasis through de-emphasis. An old trick, one of many, that seemed to only work for Morgan.

"What?"

I was getting impatient and wary.

"Well, hell Hank let's just forget what I said about 8713 for a minute and just suppose it passes somehow for any reason under the sun. The point is, we're gonna need diplomats, foreign ministers... whole bevy of treaties to work out, startin' with Mexico."

"And?" I tried to hurry Morgan toward the point.

"Well and there, since you've had such good experience with the Mexicans..." I smirked at his outdated term for Latinos, "...in your district and have done a few of those trade jaunts here and yon, I just wondered, should the need arise, if I can count on you as, uh... well, our man in Mexico so to speak. If it's needed of course," Morgan finished smiling.

"If it's needed." I allowed sarcasm to creep into my voice. The cards were on the table. I should have driven away right then but I always hung around 'til closing time. I always finished my beer. And I always had a terrible hangover because of it.

"If needed. Whaddaya say?" A winning smile that almost seemed genuine glowed on Morgan's face.

"Sure Rich, why not."

I gave in. It wasn't so much that I didn't see a way out. I had just resigned myself that Morgan would either get me or squash me and I was in no mood to be squashed.

"Well I'm glad to hear you say that, 'cause I just wanna believe that we all here can work together around our differences. I think you can be said to be a real team player Hank."

"Yeah Rich. So 8713?"

"Oh yeah right. So if we had a bit of support on 8713 that'd help us keep the Theocrats quiet, since we'd have plenty else to keep us occupied."

"I'll see what I can do."

"Thank ya Hank. Sure would be swell, a team player like you an' all. Good example, I say. Bipartisanship. Why, we could take a picture for the papers, show there's no gridlock on Texas soil." A look of lofty ideals appeared on his ancient face.

"Sure, Rich. We could do that. Mexico, ya say. You can do that too, I suppose. Ok then, 8713. I'll remember. I'll be there." I was already disappointed in myself.

"Thanks Hank.... Oh and Hank... the wife don't know where I am right now. Let's keep it that way and pretend we just kept the windows up and passed each other in the night." He winked. It made me shiver.

"Sure Rich. Goodnight."

"Night Hank."

We rolled up our windows and proceeded back down the hill in opposite directions. He headed downtown to the Governor's mansion, despite his remark about the wife. The idea of Richard Morgan fooling around with some young thing was not only highly improbable, but rather disconcerting. I went back to my hotel to phone my friend Professor Croslin in Colorado. We had met on a censorship task force under former Governor Alice Lindsay. We shared many views and my amateur interest in photography had given us a wealth of common ground. Over the years, we'd kept in touch and Croslin always made sure I knew I had a rope to climb out of the pit of Texas politics. He told me once, he'd made it his solemn oath to keep me from getting lost in the political cesspool. He always made me feel better when my job got me down, and this time the job really had me down.

When I reached the hotel, there was a message from Jack Deleo, the ABR reporter who had been hounding me and every other Texas Legislator, to give ABR an interview. Governor Morgan had 'strongly discouraged' us from talking to the press at this time and none of us were very eager to do so anyway.

I got Croslin on the phone and explained about the meeting. This time, Croslin didn't attempt to spare me.

"You screwed up, Hank. You shoulda just told him 'no' flat out. You know that. What got into you?"

"I don't know. It just seemed like there was nowhere to turn. If I didn't agree, I'd be washed out and if we do split the union I'd be washed up as well."

"You could come up to Colorado. I could use you right now. I've got a student headed to Lakota Nation to do a project. He's sharp but in a situation like this I'd feel better with an experienced chaperon of sorts. A smart man like you along to grease the wheels, not to mention your past photo experience, could help him inestimably."

"They probably wouldn't let me into the country."

"No dammit! Not after this." I could hear genuine anger rising in Croslin's voice. "Are you really gonna do it? You can still turn your back and high-tail it here. But I know you won't do that. You never run, especially when you're committed."

"And now I am truly and wholly committed." I sighed.

"Well, you should change your mind and call me. I really could use you."

I didn't know what to say except thanks. My mind was racing and nobody could make it stop. I started to think about what Morgan had actually asked me to do. Subvert my party, my constituents and the United States of America. I couldn't imagine myself doing a thing like that. But here I was feeling hog tied and impotent. There was too much at stake on the other side of the equation. Sure the grandiose, subversive stuff sounded important but what about food on the table, a career and a life. Those were important too.

I couldn't go to Colorado and leave everything I'd built here behind. Tomorrow by 2:00, I'd have to start a secession movement in my party's ranks. I got ready to do some heavy soul searching. Was the preservation of safety and security really worth it? Would I really get safety and security?

The Sun - 4

A harsh sun shone on the bankrupt land the next day. It blazed flat and white on the capitol steps in Washington, Columbia as Congressional Representatives walked to a historic vote that might avert catastrophe. And it focused like a spotlight on State Senator Hank Connely in Austin.

HANK - 2
Austin, Texas

I walked towards the bookstore on Guadalupe Street, sweating, trying to keep my mind off the present task while at the same time trying to gain peace and justification.

I entered the store and tried not to notice the steely stare of the young man behind the counter. I walked a little stiffly but straight and strong. My Momma always said my head looked like a cantaloupe with ears and brown hair stuck on it. I wore a light cotton suit, stylish but conservative gray. I certainly didn't look like a politician. The local ABR station's Latino music program played in the background. The song came to an end and the ABR news theme began to play.

"With an ABR News Nutshell, I'm Greg Whitney. Minutes ago, Congress reached a compromise over federal funding. In a hastily called press conference, the president announced martial law will end in one month. Even so, the Texas Secession Bill passed the radical House and entered the Texas Senate. Oklahoma indicated they will secede if Texas does. This has been an ABR News nutshell."

I stopped when I heard the announcement and stood near the counter listening. I looked at the clerk behind the register when it finished.

"You think they'll really do it? Secede I mean." I wondered if the general public knew how serious this was.

"Well sir, I hope not. If we're really gonna get rid of martial law, I'd say it'd be a shame to cause another crisis when there's no need to. Only the selfish would really want secession right now. Only those with something to gain."

I met his gaze. "Yeah, you're more right about that than you know."

I turned and left the store trying to forget what the clerk had said. I walked down Guadalupe St. lost to the world, my brain racing in high rationalization mode. I walked right past the El Patio Mexican Restaurant, where I was supposed to meet Bob Alvarez to talk about the prayer bill.

I walked into the University area, ignoring the hurrying students and the dragworms who had escaped the National Guard roundup and still begged for change and cigarettes. I almost got hit by a Metrobus as I tried to get across Martin Luther King Jr. Blvd. but my mind hammered away.

"I've already set things in motion. I might not be able to stop it anyway. If I try to stop it, Morgan will put a stop to my career. If I don't stop it all Hell breaks loose in Texas, I get sent to Mexico and have to live with my choice. But if I try to stop it, I may get sent out of Congress, disgraced with no way to live. I don't know how to do anything else anymore. I've already set things in motion...."

Over and over I thought, as I cut through Slusher park to the Capitol. I walked through the Capitol courtyard, noticing how aptly it reflected the royal ambitions of King Morgan. I finally began to get angry at the uncontrolled ambition of the Morgan crowd. I realized I had to stand up for once. I couldn't play this one at angles and try to squeeze through. It was all or nothing.

I stopped short and headed for the Governor's office. I rode the elevator panting, trying to control my heartbeat. I strode through the outer office, right past Kit, the receptionist and stormed in through the Governor's private office door as Kit yelled, "Mr. Connely, the Governor..."

Morgan stood looking out the window, his arms crossed behind his back. Ouida Jackson, my party Whip sat in an overstuffed chair, looking at the floor.

"Hah yew Hank?" Morgan didn't turn from the window. "Thought you was meetin' with Alvarez. No matter." He turned around and sat down in his big stuffed chair. "Me and Ouida here were just discussin' the prayer bill situation. Seems she thinks we can all get together and agree on a plan. But we're almos' done. What's on your mind Hank?" Morgan looked seriously up at me.

"Well," I started and stopped. Without doing a thing or hardly saying a word of any significance, Morgan had drained the resolve right out of me. Who was he? I hated him.

"I came to talk to you about the secession bill." I barely croaked out the words.

"Aw yeah, S.R. 8713. Ms. Jackson and I just talked over that too. Now, you know your part Hank. And with Ouida's help, it'll all be wrapped up. Pretty like a bow and everyone and everything taken care of. One big happy family."

I stood loose lipped but words hung at the back of my mind, pretending to do something else, scared to death to make their way out of my mouth.

"And you know what the best part about it is?" Morgan pointed a pen at me like a sword. "History. You, me, and you Ouida, all of us making grand history. The world watching us like an audience watches a stage. We're shaping the world. Reshaping it in our image to make a lasting mark. It's grand isn't it Ouida?" His thin lips smiled at her, not with lechery, but pure, mad grandiosity.

"Sure," Ouida agreed tentatively. "Grand is the word Governor." He did it to her too.

"All right then Hank, thanks for coming up and getting things straight. I've got a meeting at 1:30 that I need to git to. And y'all have a vote at 2:00 I think." Morgan winked at me as he put on his coat and walked out the door. I imagined tripping him and choking him as he writhed under me on the floor. Instead, I stood slack-jawed.

Ouida looked at me sneering. "Glad you came up to settle this Hank. I was having a hard time making myself understood but you really came through and laid it all down for him."

"Get off it Ouida. You and I both know this thing's going to come off through the force of Richard Morgan's personality, no matter what we do. He's either a prophet or he's crazy. Most likely he's a crazy prophet. In any case, it's best to arrange safe passage through the coming months." I had almost convinced myself. Maybe it was for the best.

"Yeah, you're right of course. I just.... I don't know. The whole thing stinks.... Do you think we could throw a wrench in it?"

I met her piercing gaze. "Yeah we could. And it'd pass anyway and we'd get thrown in the pit while Morgan barbecued brisket over us."

"Yeah. Let's go."

Ouida opened the door and we walked down to the Capitol building.

STEVE - 5
Austin, Texas

"For everything?" screeched the overlarge man with the Mighty Ducks T-shirt.

"Yes," I said, looking once more at the pile of half-rotting books, old Reader's Digest Condensed Books and dog-eared National Geographics.

The man leaned back and eyed me with a look of possible comprehension. "You mean a quarter a piece."

The man did not comprehend, and I did not reach over and grab him by the throat and carry him out of the door by his jugular.

"No, I am afraid we'll end up donating or recycling most of this. We can only give you a quarter for the lot."

The man's eyes bugged out. I didn't poke him in his bugging eyes.

"You're trying to rip me off. These old books are worth something. Look at this Bridges of Madison County. It's a classic!"

"Sir, I'm sorry but we just don't need any of this, If you have a garage sale or some friends you could give them to, you might do a little better--"

"Forget it, I'll just hold on to them. I'm not going to just give them to you...." The man trailed off muttering as he gathered the refuse back together in a box and hauled it through the back door.

"Thanks for..." the man slammed the door in my face, "...never coming in here again," I finished to myself.

I flew out the door at 5:30, and stopped at the grocery store to wander aimlessly around, reading signs. There seemed to be more signs than food.

NO GRAPES
TODAY
Due to political
troubles in
California, no
grapes were
delivered today

NO FISH
TODAY
Due to labor strikes
in the trucking
industry, no fish
were delivered
today

Fish, fruit and meats were disrupted but Pringles and peanut butter were still on the shelves. I stopped cold by the toaster pastries. I always looked for grape and vanilla fudge and they never had them. Today the shelves were filled with them. I grabbed two boxes of each.

The place was virtually empty. This grocery store used to be packed 24 hours a day. I would come at three in the morning and have to wait in a long line. Now checkout clerks sat around reading magazines. Shoppers looked furtive and restless.

I bought my pastries, a Tombstone pizza and left. I almost ran into a tanned, weathered man in a brown leather jacket as I tore out the door.

"Hey buddy can you spare a couple bucks?"

An avowed sucker, I pulled out a couple of bills.

"Thanks man, you're a right sort. So many people, a lot richer'n you won't give ya the time a day anymore. Afraid they'll get dragged away jes for helpin' a guy."

"What do you mean dragged away?" I edged away, trying not to get involved in a long conversation.

"Oh that Texas Army been 'roundin up all the homeless and vags and bussin' 'em off God knows where. Some kinda army thing, I think. Sposed to get us off the streets and make better men f'us. They won't get me though. I got an address. Cain't make ya go if ya got an address."

"Well, good luck."

"Thank ya sir." The man laughed and walked off down the parking lot, watching for cops and security agents. I dumped my groceries in the back seat and slipped behind the wheel. I turned on the radio and headed home.

"You're listening to American Belief Radio. For American Belief Radio News, I'm Jerry Martinez."

Nothing happened. The silence continued for what seemed like a half a minute. Then the announcer broke back in.

"Attention Ladies and Gentlemen. We've just received important news from the capital. In a surprise forced vote on the Texas Senate floor just minutes ago, the Texas Secession Bill passed by two votes. The Oklahoma Congress is right now voting on emergency legislation merging their legislature with the Republic of Texas. We'll have more, later in this netcast.

"Hurricane Ronald swept through southern Florida yesterday, leaving hundreds dead and thousands injured. Miami buildings were still burning and most of southern Florida was without power. The US military, already busy with federal business, has promised to provide all the troops they can spare. Residents are also receiving help from the Caribbean Alliance Countries.

"The California Peace Party reached what they called, 'a victory for community' today. The coalition of gangs and community groups obtained an agreement by Governor Yokimari to be recognized as the majority party in the State Assembly. The Peace Corps already has a majority on the Los Angeles city council. Many states criticized Governor Yokimari for dealing with terrorists."

'These are not terrorists but frustrated people. A lot of the Corps is made up of mothers and businessmen. We are dealing with the disenfranchised communities not the crime bosses. The criminals would like things to stay as they are.'

"Once again, within the last half hour, the Texas legislature sent a bill of secession to the Governor, which, if signed, would make Texas the first state to secede since 1861. Oklahoma introduced a bill which would put their state legislature under Texas' control if Governor Morgan signs the bill as expected. Also, community uprisings are reported throughout Louisiana in support of the Texas secession. Some raised the old confederate flag or the flag of Texas over post offices and courthouses.

"Finally, the South African Republic recognized the Lakota Nation today and moved to open ties with them at a meeting of the United Sovereign Nations of Africa."

KANDEL - 1
Los Angeles

I shut off the netcast and leaned back in my chair and pondered the horrible plaster job of my ceiling. I thought about Steve out in Texas. Horrible. Why he hadn't taken my invitation to join the California Peace Party I couldn't tell you, BUT, that's the way he is. Sort of conservatively arrogant and liberal. Me, I'm not like that. More down to earth, positively liberal. I do my job, which makes me feel active and good and then I go home and don't worry my conscience. That's why I signed up to the CPP's press/cultural division. I do some slightly subversive things with words, protect cultural integrity and I feel good about myself without shooting a gun or being assassinated.

The phone rang.

"Lieutenant Kandel here." I recited my title dutifully, despite the fact I abhor all the pseudo-military garbage the cultural staff has to go through. Why I even have to HAVE a title I don't know, but at least make me, reporter or editor or something, not Lieutenant.

"Hey Lieu-ten-ant." Ok, let's be honest, when Stephanie sang the title it sounded positively alluring. "Shall we celebrate the beginning of political bureaucracy with a beer and pizza."

"All right Steph. Wanna meet at your place."

"Actually, meet me at HQ. I want to show you the new command structure too."

I drove down to Hollywood and Cahuenga to meet Steph at the LA Peace Party headquarters. We still housed ourselves in the same old brick office building we started with, on the northeast corner of the intersection. The LA Peace Corps had once been small, but now that it had evolved into the California Peace Party, our little office was crammed. BUT, the higher ups thought it better to keep a continuous local profile than move into some shiny high rise complex. Besides, now we had City Hall and the Capitol for our own personal use.

The Cultural Affairs Department, which handled press relations and local cultural preservation, stuffed itself into one half of the 2nd floor. The smell was atrocious. Most of us worked from our Desksets at home, to avoid some sort of critical mass explosion that would assuredly take place if we all showed up in the office at once.

Don't get me wrong, I don't hate my job. I feel good about the things I've done. I worked hard to keep the city from bulldozing the

South Central part of the city to build an office complex. I've also done a lot of cultural work setting up community groups in the heavily Latino South Pasadena. Sometimes I felt a little weird about being the only Anglo from my sector but nobody else seems to mind.

I avoided the old double door elevator. It scared me a little. It always looked on the verge of failure. NOT that I'm claustrophobic, but I get impatient real fast. I'd go bonkers stuck in an elevator for more than five minutes.

I bounded up the stairs to the Department. I forged my way through the small decaying lunch bags, old umbrellas and power tools, into Steph's office. Steph sat facing away from the door working at her desk. She turned as soon as I burst in. She was gorgeous; long black hair and deep chestnut eyes, set narrowly on a wide face and she wore this bright pink lipstick. Like most CPP'ers she had joined to stop the violence and take control of a situation the government let get way out of hand. She joined after her parents were killed in a robbery.

I joined for different reasons. Ok, let's be honest, I'm still not sure what all of them are. It's sort of a mixture of idealism, practicality and hope. Nothing really traumatic has ever happened to me directly but man, I've seen enough shit go down that I had to do something. Practically, it keeps me on the side of the fence where I think the winners will eventually be. That may sound crass but everyone's selfish to a certain extent, whether they'll admit it or not. The LA Peace Corps was an honest, no bullshit organization and, most importantly, actually achieved something. That's as close as I'll ever get to figuring it out.

Steph greeted me just inside the door. "Hey Mark, you made good time. Come on into the Commodore's office."

Commodore. Ugh. It made me want to puke. The guy was more like president of the rotary club. I don't think the 'Commodore' had ever even seen a gun outside of the movies.

"I wanted you to see this before we eat. I think you'll be more in the mood." She leered at me, in a delightfully unnerving way.

Steph picked up a sheet of paper entitled 'California Peace Party Hierarchy' and handed it to me. She pointed to a place near the top which read 'Cultural Undersecretary Mark Kandel', then pointed to her own name next to 'Cultural Secretary'.

"Yow!" I looked at her with ecstatic bemusement "You know, I'm tired of working for you."

She eyed me mischievously. I about melted into the floor.

"Well, you could sign up for the National Guard. I mean the

California Peace Militia. I'm sure they could use another grunt on the Nevada border." She stared at me with a look that had absolutely no relation to her words.

"Nevada?"

The look of play receded from my face. This is where our relationship always hit the rocks. We should have never talked internal politics but of course, at the time, it was absolutely impossible. We had irreconcilable differences regarding the use of force. I was entirely against it but she thought it unavoidable. It was a trait I should have paid more attention to.

"Yes." She abruptly looked down. "The Militia is gathering on the border of Nevada. Purely precautionary and wholly provocative. The NPP has almost got enough votes in Carson City to repeal the party attainder the Democrats forced through and call for an alliance vote."

"So that means we're not totally demilitarizing." I cautiously tried to avoid a shouting match, which I had a history of starting. Stephanie was more the calm vicious type. I had the temper.

"Actually, yes it does. The military arm of the party will fill up the California Militia's branch of the government. Well not branch, but you know what I mean. The Peace Party now has its members in the California National Guard, just like in every other governmental office. However..."

I raised an eyebrow. I immediately wished I hadn't. Why couldn't I be sunny and encouraging? Oh don't make me sick. At least I could have been quiet though.

"Don't do that Mark. All that will happen is a few of us will go to Carson City in an advisory capacity. The NPP is absolutely capable of pulling this off on its own and is 100 percent for full integration."

"So wait. You're saying we won't be crossing the border," I ventured.

"Well, just a few of us from the peace party and--"

"And the entire California Peace Militia."

"Well not the whole thing silly, just the ones on the border. Besides, we'll be safe in Carson City and we're only cultural advisors anyway."

"Oh yes. Of course. And we all know how innocent culture is."

"Yes we do." She took the bait of my joke and tried to regain the earlier mood, "Let's go get something to eat."

We nixed the pizza and headed to the Dresden Room. A quiet cheesy atmosphere of cocktail music and faux elegance always seemed to smooth out the evening. We took a table in the corner, far away from the singing.

Stephanie visibly relaxed when we walked through the door.

"I love this place."

I took her hand. "Yeah, remember the first time we came here?"

"I was trying to recruit you."

"Yeah and I was telling you what bullshit elitist manipulators all political parties are. Imagine me being difficult."

"That's why we needed you, because you were dangerous. You could've blown the whole thing if you weren't on our side."

"Don't patronize me." I flailed at her with both hands.

She battled me off with a swizzle stick.

"You better eat that olive before you hurt someone with it." The olive drooped from the end of her swizzle stick.

"You eat it." She held it up in front of her mouth.

I leaned forward toward the olive. "Why should I? It's your olive." I half whispered. So I'm a cheese ball when it comes to romance. So what? It worked.

"Don't you want it?"

With mock puzzlement, she leaned closer, putting the olive dangerously close to her lips.

"Well if you insist."

I leaned in and met only with the kiss I'd counted on. The olive ended up on the floor. After a few minutes, I caught my breath.

"We're going to get thrown out of here for not being lonely and depressed if we keep this up."

Our dinner came and Stephanie tried to keep the conversation off the Peace Party, but I couldn't help myself. It WAS important and I couldn't just let it lie.

"I'll just be glad when all this military stuff is over. I'm not in this for banners and glory. I think it's becoming too much about status."

She leaned back and sighed. "Look Mark, you can't always complain about the hierarchy and the authority. Sometimes you just have to flow with it. When it becomes abusive, then you fight it but if the CPP had always been looking over its shoulder at its own members, it would never have California, or even L.A. We would be an ineffectual third party, like the Socialist Workers, constantly purging ourselves and arguing and never advancing, because we wouldn't trust ourselves enough to advance."

"I understand that." I really did. But it seemed like there should be some sort of middle ground. "Why do we have to move military into

Nevada? Why can't our advisors do it alone?"

I let the question stand.

She glared at me.

"You annoy the hell out of me Kandel."

Ok. I'd done it. I deserved it. But I'd stood up for my principles, right?

Stephanie's eyes drilled into my skull. "What do you want me to say? I don't control the military. You're the one who's always going on about how you're glad you're not in a position of responsibility and you just want to do your part and that's it. That's all I do. I just have a slightly bigger part that's all."

"That's fine, but it doesn't answer my question." She began to steam and I needed to press the escape valve quick. "Look, let's go to my place and get out of this smoke and lounge music."

We paid our bill and left quickly. The ride to my place was a long exercise in unpleasant silence. The 110 slid by without comment, as it narrowed into a virtual tunnel near South Pasadena.

My apartment was cut out of half a house. It had three rooms, a bathroom and a hallway that served as a kitchen.

Stephanie threw herself down on an old brown armchair underneath a poster, which portrayed the history of the CPP through bumper stickers. 'LA UNITED!' from the unification of gangs and Mafias into the Los Angeles Peace Party, which later became the CPP. 'I'M LATAFESE', from their cultural unity campaign; Latino, African, Japanese combined into one word. 'CPP AND PROP 98', from the ballot item that let the Peace Corps in as a major party. 'CPP FOR PEOPLE', from the first statewide election campaign. And, 'CPP LET'S GO', which referred to both the independence movement and the takeover of the California legislature.

Steph lit a cigarette. I walked back in the room holding a glass of whiskey.

"You want one?" She held out her cigarette.

"No. Look, I don't see why you can't see my point about the hierarchy and the military. This is supposed to be a people's party and here we are, forcing the Governor of Nevada, practically at gunpoint, to hand the state over to us so we can take over and then what? Oregon? Washington?"

"Of course not, the Peace Parties aren't strong enough and you know that. Wait!" She stopped me before I started in on her last statement. "And we won't interfere in any state where the Peace Party doesn't have the support of the people. Taking Nevada isn't a military operation. The military is only needed to keep the moneyed interest from crushing the NPP initiative."

"Ok, so it's not meant to be evil. But guns man, I just don't go for that."

I plopped down in front of her on the floor, leaned back, and she began to massage my shoulders. A subtle argumentative ploy, but one I enjoyed.

I thought back to why she had bothered to recruit me in the first place. We met on a bus and somehow fell to talking. I was fanatically cynical at the time and she tried to show me that something good could be accomplished. The CPP was doing it. I of course, resisted her completely and this argument was one in a series dating from that first one. Her optimistic idealism clashed pretty hard sometimes with my more cynical brand.

"Poor guy." Her soft words fell pleasantly against my neck.

"Yeah, I know, I've got it rough. I'm on the inside and have a 98% chance of being behind the guns. Maybe I'd feel differently..."

She was tired of listening to me and knew the one way to shut me up. Her arms slipped down my sides and she slid behind me on the floor. I mean come on, sometimes denial is fun right?

"You're making it difficult to compose political theories... uhhh."

I turned around to face her and the political talk stopped for the night.

STEVE - 6
Austin, Texas

In an attempt to assess the possibility of legally leaving Texas, I spent the day running down citizenship information for myself and Helen. I left the Department of Human Services bleary eyed and worn out. The new Republic of Texas rules about citizenship affected even the most mundane things like parking and paying your water bill. When I got home, I shut the door and fell down on the floor of the apartment.

After staring at the ceiling for ten minutes, I finally decided to absorb some mindless entertainment. I turned on the Deskset and skimmed video servers, until I caught a rerun of a nighttime talk show.

"And you'll never believe this, a special report leaked out today. It seems the Texas secession is being backed by Dallas Cowboys Coach Fred Smartin. Yes, he figures he can FINALLY get a National Championship if he only has to play Houston and San Antonio." The audience laughed.

I clicked to the next channel as Helen came through the door.

"How did it go?" I genuinely feared the response.

"Rotten."

Her eyes looked nowhere in particular. She huffed and puffed into the kitchen and set down a grocery bag.

"I picked up some onions, chicken and chipotle sauce to make Tenga. I figured I needed to treat myself to something. I also got a nice Chianti."

"Wasn't it strange how empty the store was?"

"Oh, you mean the fruit and stuff?" She whisked off into the next room.

"Yeah that too." I stood up to make myself more available for conversation, "But I mean there were hardly any people shopping. There was nobody in line."

"Yeah I didn't think about it but I guess you're right." She unloaded the groceries with a little too much fervor.

I helped her put things away and gingerly approached the subject we were both avoiding. "So what happened at the employment place?"

"Absolutely nothing. All of us sat in the outer office of the employment commission, holding our little green tickets and no one spoke to us until 5 o'clock when they told us to leave and come back tomorrow."

"They didn't tell you anything else?"

Helen slammed a can of tomatoes down and looked at the counter top. She sighed and her voice began to shake.

"Steve I don't want to talk about it.... O.K. I cried all the way to the grocery store... and if..."

I came up and quickly put my arms around her. She sobbed on my shoulder for a few minutes.

"I'm sorry." She whimpered just the way I hated.

"It's ok. I asked Kip at work about that lead he had with the UN provisional staff. He gave me a number."

"I'm never going to a get a job with them. Not with a degree in Art History and a half finished Geology Master's."

"Look, your years in management at the library will count big with these people. They're going to need someone good with information resources that they won't have to pay librarian salaries. Besides, the fact that you're not 'Texan' will work FOR you in this case." I didn't really believe anything I was saying but it seemed important not to let Helen's hopes sink.

She looked up at me with hopeless eyes. "Speaking of which, did you find out if we have to get married?"

"Yes... We don't. As long as you're on the lease with me, a working Texan, you're fine. Besides, since you were born in Texas I think you'll be higher on the list of citizenship. In any case, we may not want to get locked in here. I'm considered a friendly foreign national of the State of Illinois and am free to go whenever I want. As long as you don't have citizenship that makes it easier for you to go with me."

Helen stared at me. Her eyes glistened with tears and her lower lip stuck out.
"Why can't they just leave us alone?"

"They have been. For too long."

I squeezed her tight, then moved away quickly, in case she caught the tiny amount of insincerity growing in my actions. I punched up the news netcast without thinking how she might respond.

"More and more Parishes in Western Louisiana are declaring themselves part of the Republic of Texas. President Richard Morgan welcomed them into the newly formed Republic. Louisiana's legislature voted by a slim margin to allow Parishes self-determination.

"The African Sovereign Nations recognized the Lakota Nation today. The Lakota also agreed on a permanent cease-fire with the US government. UN regional negotiator, Alaine Pascual, reached the settlement by allowing the US to claim oversight rights while guaranteeing the Lakota complete sovereignty.

"The President delivered a special address after the signing."

"And it proves we can peacefully, and without bloodshed settle our differences and move ahead to the betterment of all."

(Beeeeeeeeeeeeeeeeeeeeeeeeeeeeeeeeeeeeeeeeeeeeeeeeeeeep)

"This is not a test. This is not a test. Citizens of the states of Arkansas and Kansas are advised to seek shelter and stay indoors. Do not join the fighting except to defend your own living area. Do not take up arms. The US Army is providing assistance to local National Guardsmen. Stay sheltered and indoors until further notice."

(Beeeeeeeeeeeeeeeeeeeeeeeeeeeeeeeeeeeeeeeeeeeeeeeeeeeep)

"This is American Belief Radio. Reports are coming in that the Republic of Texas has opened fire on US troops in Texarkana, Fort Smith and Fayetteville Arkansas as well as Wichita, Kansas. Jack Wilson is in Fayetteville."

A voice crackled over the sounds of gunfire and explosions.

"Yes, Greg, I don't know how much time I'll have. We were staying in a motel here on State Line Road...US-71, which runs along the Texas border, when suddenly, without any warning, the whole strip came under mortar fire." The reporter began to cough. "All the guests ran away from the highway and we're now hunkered down in the basement of some friendly Texarkanans. The most dreadful... uh, the most dreadful moment came when about five fire trucks, responding to various alarms came screaming up the road and were all hit by the shelling. Texarkana at this point is missing a large part of its fire department and there are fires visible all over this part of the city."

"Any idea why the heavy use of artillery?" Whitney interjected.

"Well," Wilson said thank you to someone off mike. "Well Greg, no. I guess," he laughed, "that's about as clear as I'm going to get. I just got handed a sheet." A large blast ripped through my speakers. "We're going to have to get moving again... I just got handed a sheet that lists an estimated 30 dead, 17 of those were under 18 and 45 injuries reported from the hospital. Those numbers seem odd to me but I don't think anything is operating smoothly here right now." Another blast came over the speakers followed by the sound of plaster falling. "Listen Greg, we're out of here now. The family's dragging me out the door. From Texarkana, Arkansas, Jack Wilson reporting."

"Thanks Jack and our thoughts are with you. The Texas Army has moved into Arkansas and Kansas. We have no official reports of any kind but Texarkana and Wichita seem to be receiving the heaviest shelling. The Texans apparently were expecting heavy resistance in those towns.

"In addition, the California Militia has reportedly entered Nevada to aid the Nevada Peace Party. No shooting has been reported there. The Nevada governor fled the capitol and the Peace Party members of the Nevada legislature voted to suspend Congress until further notice."

KOLBRASKI - 3
East St. Louis, Illinois, Eastbound I-70

I almost ran the car off the road. I turned to Rob Gehrig whom I'd picked up from work downtown.

"Did they say what I thought they said?"

"Yep, Texas is invading Arkansas and Kansas." Gehrig almost sounded giddy. "And California must be invading Nevada."

"Peacefully, of course." I couldn't hold back my sarcasm. "Man, this is getting too close."

"I know." The St. Louis Arch slowly sank beneath a hill behind us. "If they get past Little Rock, nothing will stop them till they get here."

"Via Memphis."

I silently calculated to myself. This changed a lot. It was time.

"Yeah, I wonder which one they'll destroy first?" Gehrig wondered aloud.

"Neither."

Gehrig threw a look at me. He freaked when I talked like that but it had to be done. We went to High School together in Greenville and had known each other almost all our lives. Gehrig had trained in criminology. Some of the best times we'd had were just sitting around drinking and arguing about Philosophy, Psychology and Politics. Ever since I joined the Ozarkians, we'd had less to talk about. I thought my secrecy was for his own good, but the Texans marching up the river changed a lot.

He looked at me without realizing his life would soon change. It was both our fates. "Are you coming over for poker tonight?" Such an innocuous question from a man about to lose his innocence.

"No, I've got a meeting." I saw that he felt the horrible import of my words.

"Another Psych Association thing?"

"Yeah, and I...I think you should come." There I'd done it. No turning back now. Gehrig was in part way, whether he wanted to or not. But what was I all flipped about. The Feds weren't paying any attention to us. We had people way up in the St. Louis Board of Aldermen and even the Mayor tacitly approved of us.

"Why should I come?" I could tell he was apprehensive.

"Because it's... we need you.... I mean your perspective on the criminal mind and the use of firearms would be good. John will be there." I tried to get close to the truth without really saying anything. It sounded stupid, but I suddenly felt if I could get Gehrig to come on his own, then somehow I wouldn't have to feel responsible.

"I have a degree in criminology and can shoot a gun. That does not sound like the requirements for a Psych Association."Gehrig searched for more information.

I stared at Gehrig, gaging him. I knew he was too smart to be led blindly. I also knew if I told him about the Ozark Defense Group that I could never let him out. I never recruited my friends, only strangers who had inquired about the organization through various channels. But I knew Gehrig, and knew he was smarter than his low-paying job. He could shoot a gun and shoot it well. Rob's advisor at the University of Illinois wanted him to go on to graduate work in Criminology because he was so good with strategy. I knew all this and knew, that despite and because of the risk, we needed Gehrig.

"The Psychology Association has a few members that meet afterward, Rob. We're part of a group known as Ozarkia. It's a network of militias across the Ozark area which are right now drawing battle plans to defend the area against Big Brother Texas." I kept my eyes on the road, ready for any kind of response.

Gehrig stared straight ahead and said nothing.

"I've already told you too much by telling you that, Rob," I continued. "If you don't want in, tell me now and all I ask is that you NEVER mention this again. Even if you do I'll deny it and someone will pay you back." I feared that the most.

Gehrig continued to stare ahead. After a big ol' silence he finally said, "I'm in."

JEFF - 2
Denver, Colorado

"Now Jeff, this isn't going to be like Central America, even Belize." Professor Croslin leaned forward towards me. He filled his suit but wasn't fat. He had curly black hair and round glasses. When he leaned forward, it was kind of like having a pile driver waved in your face.

"This is a technologically advanced and well-developed area. They are literate and not really poor at all. In fact, you could say it's the reverse of Central America because the US is, in a sense, the one being oppressed not doing the oppressing... for once." He made one of his characteristic dramatic feints with a finger and leaned back in his chair.

I nodded and looked out the window at the students hustling back and forth to class, amid the oranges and browns of fall. "I've heard that they treat everyone fairly equally though."

I was afraid Croslin would back out of the program at any moment. I was also trying to get him to let me take Faye along. I felt uneasy leaving her behind in Colorado. More than that, I envisioned us having a wonderful, exciting and maybe even hair-raising time, bouncing around in the Lakota Nation, you know. I wasn't going to let Croslin get me down.

Croslin was going on about the egalitarianism of the Lakota. "Still, it's hard to say. The word from my friends at SDU who can still get on the net, is that if you accept Lakota sovereignty, you're fine but if you're emigrating or are stupid enough to move to a reservation, then you really get rode hard by everyone. You can see why I'm concerned about sending you, a citizen of the US, in there. Especially since you're a photographer, which always carries ominous overtones to a young government or insurrectionary force."

"The assignment has changed then."

"Yes my young master of the understatement, the assignment has changed." Croslin leaned forward again. "But not entirely. You're still focusing on local culture and customs in the Black Hills, but the culture has changed the assignment from a breeze way to spend grant money, into one hell of an opportunity to document history."

I suppressed a grin and looked straight into Professor Croslin's eyes. I knew Croslin admired me. He lived vicariously through me to a certain extent. If I played it cool enough, I might just nudge him into letting Faye come.

"I guess I don't mind."

Croslin smirked, "All right Jeff, you get your cool self off to that party."

"Are you coming?" I put on my backpack and stepped behind the small wooden swivel chair I'd been sitting in. I hoped he would. Faye and I could work on him tag-team in the more pliable atmosphere of the party.

"I'll be there late. There are a few things I have to take care of at the Dean's office. They don't want you to go alone. I'll work it out."

"Faye could really help me out on this," I ventured, holding my breath. "She's been out on shoots enough times before and really was an asset, you know."

"Normally, you know, I wouldn't mind. I respect your friend Faye very much. But this is somewhat of a danger spot. The University doesn't want to take on more liability than it must with this."

"So, she'll come along anyway."

"The Lakota Nation might have something to say about that. Now out. I've got work to do."

"Ok, see you tonight."

I biked down to the departmental party at Professor Jones' house. Laughter and murmuring poured out of the windows. Professor Jones barely held on to a position at the University, often calling in sick to class the day after his parties. However, when he did show up, he espoused some of the most brilliant theories on aesthetics that the department had ever heard. I noticed Faye's bike as I locked mine up and hurried inside.

Music, smoke and chatter floated toward me through the front door. In the Victorian mansion-like front room, a group of five people, including Faye, gathered around a Deskset. It and a large overstuffed lime green chair with the word 'Nirvana' embroidered on it, were the only objects in the room.

"Heyyy," smiled Faye as she sauntered over to me. "All us geeks are just waitin' for the news." Faye wore a white dress with little red ribbons. She called it her Terry Spellman outfit, after the popular actress. I usually teased her about it, just to watch her pretend not to care. I let it go this time.

"What else is shakin'?"

Faye sucked on a beer while she talked. "Not much. Did you get the trip stuff worked out?"

"Yeah, I'm gonna make them let me take you with me."

"For sure?" A slight hope hid behind her eyes. I loved her eyes.

"Not for sure but damned close. Maybe you should use your womanly wiles when Croslin shows up--"

Faye smacked me gently. "SHHH, the interview's starting. It's some big shot from Harvard, who everyone here thinks is gonna tell Jack Deleo to shove it or something."

"It's 9 o'clock Eastern Standard Time and this is American Belief Radio's America in Crisis. I'm Jack Deleo. Thanks for joining us. Our guest this evening is Dr. Jaime Mantagua, a professor of political science at Harvard University in Massachusetts. He'll join us in just a moment. First the news."

"For American Belief Radio News I'm Greg Whitney.

"Another trouble spot flared up in the west today. A coalition of white supremacists in Lewiston, Idaho declared the Aryan Nation independent. The Aryans claim a vast territory that stretches into parts of Washington, Montana and Oregon. Idaho State officials confirm that the group only holds any power in Lewiston, Idaho and the surrounding Mountains. The uprising comes only a few days after the Montana government reached a settlement with Prophetcor, a cult group which owns a large amount of land in rural Montana.

"Utah passed a bill today making secession automatic if Nevada secedes from the US. Nevada is currently dominated by the so-called Peace Party, which has unofficially united California and Nevada as a republic.

"Wichita, Kansas received more shelling from Texas Militia troops, who are trying to capture that town for the Texas Republic. In Wichita, Jack Wilson has more."

Jack Wilson began shouting from the field over the sound of gunfire.

"Lately the names of Sarajevo, Beirut and Stalingrad quite often pass the lips of the besieged residents of Wichita. The people, who at one time were loud supporters of American Nationalism, now feel abandoned and betrayed by the federal government. Residents do not understand why there has been no US Army to meet the Texans. In the meantime, the town has no money for hospitals, schools or police, which are badly needed now. Still, the frontier spirit lives in this city, as its volunteer militia bravely holds off the Texans. Pride once directed at the nation is now directed at their own children, as they fight... and sometimes die... protecting the city. In Wichita, Kansas, Jack Wilson reporting."

"Thanks Jack. On the other front, the Texans met little resistance in Arkansas, as they continued their march towards Little Rock.

"Finally, the gangs that control Chicago and Detroit signed a pact which aims to unite the two groups in a city-state alliance. Mayor Daley of Chicago, called the act repulsive and evil. He spoke from his temporary headquarters in Springfield, Illinois. For American Belief Radio, I'm Greg Whitney."

"This is America in Crisis. I'm Jack Deleo. With me is Dr. Jaime Mantagua of Harvard University, a political scientist. Thank you for being with us Dr. Mantagua."

"My pleasure."

"There have been many analyses of the trouble in the west but the most difficult problem seems to be Texas. How serious are they and what demands must be met to stop them?"

"They're very serious Jack. They're using guns after all. They're shooting people. Killing people. I believe that's about as serious as you can get. I don't think anything will stop them."

A stunned silence dragged on while Jack collected himself.

"Are you saying that we are experiencing some kind of permanent dissolution here, uh..."

"Absolutely. People have to quit hiding their heads in the sand. The Federal Government of the US is broke. States have had to shoulder more and more of the burden of government, until states like Texas have learned to get along without the federal government. The military law and threat of organized violence has scared most states into drastic action. Texas is just capable of taking more drastic action than some others."

Deleo paused again.

"Well, then, surely the same does not apply to the Lakota or California."

"I don't see why not. The Lakota crisis could have been avoided but the US mismanaged it. That has given popular groups, like the California Peace Party, the courage to act. It's becoming a question of survival for states. If the power gap of the federal government is left to be filled by community groups, like in California and Chicago, states risk dissolution. I wouldn't be surprised to see more moves like Utah's and more state coalitions for mutual protection."

The show continued with Jack Deleo trying to hold on to the idea that the US could not possibly break apart. The doctor simply returned to his thesis of ineffective federal government and the pressures of crime.

Callers seemed to back up Mr. Mantagua, if they were from areas outside the east coast. With the Lakota uprising stabilized and the US confined to the Sioux Falls area, people already seemed comfortable with their new homelands. The show took calls from people in places they identified as Pierre, Lakota Nation and Oklahoma City, Texas. People in Texas were belligerent and blamed the US for Texas' secession. Most people calling from the Lakota Nation waxed eloquently about the improvement of the government there.

After finishing our informal analysis of the talk show, we abandoned ourselves to the party. I vowed to myself not to bring up the Lakota trip, for fear of cursing it. Even when Professor Croslin showed up later, we said very little about it.

Eventually, as usual, Professor Jones cornered me. I stood next to the Deskset and he stood blocking any avenue of escape. He held a Budweiser and went on about the Eurojazz show now coming over ABR.

"Because the People don't have any control over it that's why. Now you take..." He paused while his eyes rolled around in his head looking for the rest of the sentence. "You take the band.... Have you ever heard of a 1990's band called Nirvana?"

Here we go again. Professor Jones, despite his incredible intellect, was fascinated with a late 20th century garage band called Nirvana. If allowed, he would lecture me for hours on all their finer points. I braced myself and wished for a tornado, blizzard or some other act of God to deflect him from his train of thought. We had been having a great conversation about cultural icons and their increasing diversified nature amongst social subgroups. I racked my brain for a way to distract him. Damn! His beer was full. No hope there. At least not for the next five minutes.

"Nirvana was the first band... ever..." He took a swig. Bigger, I encouraged him in my mind. Bigger swigs. Drink man drink.

"The first band... ever..."

Suddenly the Deskset saved me. The Eurojazz show that had inspired Professor Jones to his Nirvana reverie cut off abruptly and was replaced by a loud emergency news announcement. Everyone shut up, even Jones.

"We interrupt for an American Belief Radio News emergency update. Let's join Jack Wilson in Little Rock, Jack?"

Motors revved and trucks rolled over gravel as Jack Wilson brought another report from the field. He was either superhuman or his previous report from a half an hour earlier had been taped, because he was now live from Little Rock.

"Thank you Jerry. I'm actually outside Little Rock, in Camp Joseph T. Robinson, where militias from Arkansas and Missouri and even some troops from Kentucky and Illinois are amassing in what, until now, was a secret alliance of peoples of the Ozarks. No official statement has been made but it seems several regions in Northern Arkansas and Southern Missouri are banding together to fight the Texas onrush, which until now has met no resistance in this small state. In Little Rock, Arkansas, Jack Wilson reporting."

"Thank you Jack. The US government refuses to comment but seems to be granting the Ozark coalition tacit support. The Texas government dismissed the coalition, stating Texas is not at war but simply moving into territory that considers itself part of Texas. They point to the previous lack of resistance as evidence of this. American Belief Radio will keep you up to date as more information becomes available. This has been an emergency report from American Belief Radio news."

"Damn ABR." Professor Jones couldn't hide his disgust. "They faked that earlier report from Wichita for cheap effect. Bullshit. The trouble with ABR...."

His words were drowned out by a plane flying low overhead.

GEHRIG - 1
Camp Joseph T. Robinson

Throughout the entire flight, Kolbraski drilled me on the rites and rituals of the Ozarkian structure. My mind wandered. The Ozarkians were fanatically ritualistic. I would have to take an oath when we landed. If I couldn't recite it from memory, I wouldn't be allowed into the Army.

Kolbraski droned on in a schoolmaster's tone, "There are four divisions to Ozarkia and six political parties. You won't have to worry about party affiliation just yet but I'll tell them you're with me in the Ozark People's Coalition. It's the right leaning middle group."

We deplaned in Camp Robinson and headed for the processing desk.

Kolbraski approached the man sitting behind the desk. "Platonic Republican. O.P.C. Coordinator First Class Mack E. Kolbraski."

The man seemed to recognize Kolbraski. "Right. Who's this?"

"This is former US citizen Robert Boone Gehrig. Unassigned. Temporary O.P.C. No rank."

"Will he swear the resistance oath?"

The situation overwhelmed me and I could barely squeak out a reply.

"Raise your right hand and repeat the oath from memory."

"We, the peoples of the Ozarks, with mutual respect for creed and beliefs of all people herein, do resist the oppression and disrespect of any force which attempts to poison and destroy our way of life. We commit ourselves to... to... comp... combat and eradicate those forces from the domain of the Ozark peoples."

Kolbraski let out a sigh. He wouldn't have to send me back to St. Louis.

"Right," the processor barked, "Take him to five."

The Ozark People's Coalition assigned me the rank of Coordinator 2nd class/Driver to serve in Kolbraski's unit. All recruits served with their recruiter for the first few weeks to deter any espionage and put the responsibility for the recruit's actions in the hands of the recruiter.

As I finished suiting up in a small barracks area, Kolbraski swaggered in. "You gonna be ready to hit the road soon?"

"Sure. Why waste time?"

"That's it. Uh, I've gotta get ready to brief the unit... and Gehrig... I won't have time to train you on recovery. That means if we get split up or captured, all I can say is keep your eyes peeled and get out. Better yet, let's just not GET captured, Driver."

I nodded and smiled. I was happy with the amount of confidence Kolbraski showed in me. He had implicit faith in all people until he had reason to believe otherwise. I finished suiting up and headed across the camp to the briefing room. The Ozarkians looked like an army, in as much as they had military hardware. They wore military uniforms of many different styles. Some even wore firefighter or police uniforms and others just had on whatever felt most comfortable. They had given me a green O.P.C. uniform that consisted of a green Oxford worn unbuttoned over a black T-shirt and black jeans.

I stopped and watched an older woman giving orders to a group hoisting a car out of a ditch. White-hot spirit infected each one of them as they heaved the old Buick back onto the road. They didn't look overworked, hard pressed or discouraged. They looked determined. That's what they had that the Texan army didn't. They believed in what they did, right down to the last soldier. Even if it didn't work, the Ozarkians couldn't really lose.

The other 13 people in Kolbraski's unit lounged in a conference room. John was with them and waved for me to come sit next to him. I sat down and only had time to exchange a brief greeting with him before Kolbraski walked in and started the briefing.

The First Southern Illinois Ozarkians, the only unit from Illinois, would deploy at the northern rim of Little Rock. We would raise diversionary cane while the St. Louis Elite Ozarkians flanked the Texans and moved closer in.

"All right folks, that's it. Gehrig will drive my car. We're strapped for good drivers and he's trained in cop driving so we can count on him. No worries." Kolbraski noticed the group looked worried anyway. "Listen, I let him drive me in rush hour traffic many times. There was gunfire then too."

Everyone laughed.

Our unit had three unmarked sedans modified with bulletproof exteriors and rifle slots. The gunners for my car assembled and introduced themselves to me as they got in.

A man with shaggy brown hair and a lanky build spoke first. "I'm Kelly Hutchinson from El Dorado, Illinois but everybody calls me Hutch. I'm the car marksman. Let's go get 'em."

"Shut up Hutch." A man peered out from behind him grinning. "I'm Marty Cantrill. Good to meet you. Don't let Hutch's professional manner get you down. He can actually shoot." John got in the back seat with Hutch and Cantrill. I swung around to the driver's side and Kolbraski got in the front passenger seat.

I drove the lead car out of the gate and on to Camp Robinson Road.

"Turn here." Kolbraski barked orders at me but I reacted pretty naturally for being thrown directly into combat. I had trained in firearms and criminal pursuit driving and had extensive experience in outdoor war games and reenactments. In a way the whole thing wasn't real to me. It seemed like a weekend out on the simulator.

I spun the wheel into a desolate suburban development. We drove a few miles and began to receive gunfire from a shopping center. Our three cars spread out into side streets and parking lots and began shooting up whatever we could find.

I rammed the car into the side of a Pizza Hut and the others began clearing the building of windows.

"I HATED working for them," I yelled. I already felt high on the excitement.

"Yeah but their bread sticks were good." Cantrill shouted over the engine.

Something caught Kolbraski's eyes and he cut the banter short. "Snipers in the Cosmetics shop! Take her around Gehrig."

I drove along the sidewalk by the Cosmetics shop. Glass burst in front of us, as a tank rolled out of a Walgreen's.

"Shit!" I turned hard left, squealing the tires.

Kolbraski's rasping voice barely rose above the din. "Floor it south! It'll take them a minute to get up to speed!"

"They weren't supposed to have tanks!"

"Yeah, Hutch, well, we don't pour a ton of money into intelligence reports do we." Kolbraski turned his attention back to the battle.

The tanks took awhile to get rolling and I was sure I could get out of range. I sped through the empty parking lot, avoiding the cement barriers and opening up a good distance. The sun set and streetlights began to come on.

I took us away from the tanks, our gunners shooting out streetlights. A green truck appeared directly in front of me and I swung the car hard into a side street. I smiled at the thrill of the chase and caught Kolbraski looking at me wide-eyed. I looked up to see a brick wall meet the front of our sedan.

STEVE - 7
Austin, Texas

"Ok. I'm going."

Helen put on her backpack.

"Right." I got up to kiss her goodbye.

Helen looked tired. Her eyes drooped and her shoulders drooped and her asthma had been getting worse. Her only job lead, the UN job had disappeared when the Republic banned the UN provisional staff. There seemed to be nothing left for her but to get out. I was trying like mad to do just that. Mulu was on the case.

"It'll get better." I stroked her hair reassuringly. "And if it doesn't get better we'll make it get better. I've been thinking we'll have to do something. And we can, so don't get all down. Ok?" I smiled and hugged her. She nodded and we kissed again.

I didn't believe 25 percent of what I'd just told her. Simone popped into my mind involuntarily. It happened all the time. What if I would have left Helen for her. Maybe I'd be in New Mexico with her now instead of Sam. Not that I begrudged Simone to Sam. They were perfect for each other. But ever since my 'fling' with Simone two years ago, my relationship with Helen had become much rockier.

I decided it was best not to dwell on things like that. It only made things worse. Helen could sense when I had been thinking about it and it usually led to an ugly, passive aggressive scene.

I went over to the Deskset and decided to check my mail. There was a message from Mark Kandel, whom I hadn't heard from since before the budget crisis. I wondered now what would've happened if I'd moved out to L.A. Mark had been really hot on getting me out there.

I told myself to stop the 'what would've happened' stuff. I wasn't that unhappy with Helen.

There's no way I would have ever gone to California anyway. I just didn't believe in organizations like the CPP. I was surprised Mark had joined. Mark had always believed more in direct action than I had but Mark was also a fierce individualist. I wondered how Mark got along in a martial organization like the CPP.

There was the time back in Illinois, when Mark worked for me, that he began saluting everyone at work and wearing military garb. He reached the limit when he began blasting military marches and referring to the General Manager as Herr Director. I barely saved his ass from the

GM. I saved Mark's ass at that netradio station quite often. I was really glad I didn't have to anymore. I missed the radio days but I didn't miss the aggravation.

Mark's message popped up on screen.

```
TO:steven@retail.hpb.com
FROM:UCMauer@culture.cpp.pol
RE:All this jazz.

STEVE! Crazy ain't it. I'm no longer a
Lieutenant, I'm now Undersecretary of Culture
which means, well of what I can tell you, that
I'm in charge of all press and media liaisons
and releases. Harmless really but a steady job.
I mean, we just took over a large western
state. Can't be all bad. Things are movin'
though gotta run. I'll let you know when it's
clear to come visit, if the Texans will let you
out.

Mark
```

Not funny. They might not. The border controls were getting stricter. The Texans didn't want anyone leaving or entering the country while the war rolled on. They felt that was the best way to insure security. Of course, everyone was still free to go anywhere they wanted. Of course, if you tried to cross the border there would suddenly be a fee you hadn't paid, or your insurance magically expired, or your license was no longer applicable, or your flight had been indefinitely canceled.

Still with the help of Mulu in Denton, I thought we might slip across into Oklahoma. Although it was part of Texas, it was easier to get across an Oklahoma border than a Texas one. Mostly because there were small wars raging on most of Oklahoma's borders. We had to visit Mulu soon.

The next message came from Kolbraski.

```
TO:steven@retail.hpb.com
FROM:PlatosPal@kennedy.siue.edu
RE:Uhhh...

Can't tell you much but I'm leaving Greenville
for a while and don't know when or if I'll be
back. Gehrig's coming with me. We'll drop a
```

```
line somewhere, hopefully. Later.

Kolby.
```

I didn't like the tone or implications of that message at all. It finally dawned on me that Kolbraski must be involved in this Ozarkian thing in some way. Of course. He always went on about Plato and Nietzsche and the need for resistance. It made perfect sense. The last message was from Frank Lankel, my friend who lived in Chicago. I'd been worried about him and hadn't been able to get a hold of him. I didn't recognize his new address.

```
TO:steven@retail.hpb.com
FROM:FLankel@security.Ohare.aaf.gov
RE: This will be read

Hey, guess what. I'm workin for the man who
took down the man. I'm checking security
people. I don't get any vacation time so if you
come up to Chicago be sure to stop in and say
hi. Hope the Texans aren't maiming you like
they're doing to us here. Sell the children.

Frank
```

I almost wrote Frank to explain that I hoped we'd be flying through Chicago soon and would let him know. I thought better of it. It made me angry that I couldn't reply the way I wanted. I got up and paced around. We had to get away from Texas. Soon. In the back of my mind, I'd thought maybe we could get by and get out after the war. No way. Not only couldn't I stand the idea of the Texas Republic but Helen was in danger. The stress of the situation was wearing away at our relationship too.

I browsed through message boards. Every posting had something to do with the current state of upheaval. I found a rewrite of Route 66. ROUTE 66 MAIN STREET USA/CHICAGO/OZARKIA/TEXAS/CALIFORNIA

IF YOU PLAN TO MOTOR WEST WITH EASE TRAVEL MY WAY TAKE THE HIGHWAY THAT'S UNDER SIEGE GET YOUR KICKS ON ROUTE 66

IT WINDS FROM CHICAGO TO L.A.
ALTHOUGH CHICAGO SECEDED YESTERDAY
WATCH OUT FOR TROOPS ON ROUTE 66
NOW YOU GO THROUGH ST. LOUIE
JOPLIN, OZARKIA
OKLAHOMA CITY IS PART OF TEXAS NOW
SEE AMARILLO
AVOID SHOTS IN GALLUP NEW MEXICO
FLAGSTAFF, CALIFORNIA
IF NOT YET, I WARN YOU
KINGMAN, BARSTOW, SAN BERNARDINO ARE PART
OF THE CPP'S TIMELY PLAN
TO CHOP 66 UP ACROSS THE LAND
DON'T GET SHOT ON ROUTE 66

I messed around some more and clicked over to the ABR netcast.

"A coalition of militias in the northern regions of Arkansas and Southern Missouri have declared themselves independent. The so-called People's Republic of the Ozarks say they formed to fight the invasion of Arkansas by Texas.

"In a surprise move, the United Nations granted the Lakota Nation conditional recognition. The UN calls it a gesture of good will towards the upstart nation, which unlike the Texas Republic, has pursued mostly peaceful means to end its conflict with the US.

"The governor of Utah signed legislation granting special powers to any group which can defend its borders. The California Peace Corps is occupying Nevada, placing troops along the borders of Utah and Arizona.

"And finally, Montana formed a coalition of state militias and police forces to battle the Aryan Nation in northern Idaho and deter further Lakota expansion. Idaho and Wyoming, joined Montana in the coalition."

KANDEL - 2
Carson City, Nevada

"There's no way that story can release! Of course.... well first of all the government behind that is useless.... Amend your own damned constitution then, all I'm saying is.... Shut up! I'm telling you that unless you want a public panic in Reno with a bunch of thugs and looting JUST LIKE TEXAS... you'd better hold that story. It's not censorship......yeah... listen, print that story and a town's ruination and all the death and destruction that go with it are on your head."

I slammed down the phone. "Carol, get me the stat sheets on last night's netcasts."

"Slow down honey, we only got one state here." Stephanie patted my head as she breezed by.

"Thanks." I grabbed the stat sheets. "Hey, Vince? Can we get ABR on the line? Their netcast rating is sky-high and they're calling this a takeover."

"Consider it done." Vince immediately picked up a phone

Stephanie popped her head back into the room. "Mark. Can I see you for a minute?"

"Yes?"

It was the first time either of us had talked privately in two solid days. I walked into her office and closed the door. I hate that feeling when you've both been having conversations in your head with each other but haven't talked, so you don't know really where anything stands. She sat down and began poring over some papers.

"Look. I know it's busy but couldn't we take a break..." I looked at her imploringly.

"Yes, I miss you too but," she sighed, "I've got some disturbing intelligence here."

"I've always admired your intelligence."

"No sweetheart, these reports." She waved toward a collection of papers. "According to them, there's a high probability of riots in Arizona and New Mexico."

"And that could mean Southern Cal too?" I settled down to business.

"And Texas." She looked hard at me.

"War?"

"Well, the other part of the report says Texas is planning to invade

New Mexico and Arizona to 'protect' them if riots do break out. CPP central decided we should assist Arizona in such a case and block Texas from taking anything past New Mexico."

"So we're talking a police action."

"Nope, just taking over Arizona."

"Permanently?"

"That depends on UN reaction. They haven't even talked about us yet so we have no idea how they'll interpret it. But we've decided to cooperate with them, unlike Texas."

"So in other words, we'll hold Arizona for the UN. They'll give us a chunk of desert in thanks and send us back down I-10."

"And guess who gets to handle the cultural affairs?" She smiled like a plastic clown.

My eyes shriveled up inside my head. A low moan escaped from somewhere near my intestines. I didn't like how nonchalantly, Stephanie was handling our upcoming separation.

"Yes, honey. Be careful out there. And I MEAN that. The Arizona Peace Party is extremely small and unpopular but it's our 4th largest behind Washington State's. You'll have a hookup in Tucson. A unit of advance militia folks and the entire APP at your disposal. Your main task is to meet with the Native American group there and try to secure some kind of cooperative agreement."

"Wait, that's Diplomacy's job not Culture."

"They threw it to Culture because they're short staffed in Diplomacy and part of it is a cultural matter with the Native Americans."

I nodded my head. "Yeah, I guess I can see that. When do I leave?"

"Tonight."

"Tonight?!" My shriek made her look away. Too quickly for my liking. I had a hard time keeping the wild banshees from my voice. "Who recommended me for this?"

"Central wanted someone from Cultural and told me I couldn't be spared, so we just went down the line."

"So you recommended that I be sent away into a danger zone for an indefinite amount of time. That's what happened. You can't deny it."

"No Mark, don't look at it that way."

"What WAY am I supposed to look at it? This Nevada thing is a great excuse for avoiding me. Maybe I'm overreacting but it seems like we could have caught a few minutes here and there and--"

"Look Mark, if you're going to be like this, maybe one of us should...I don't know, listen Mark, the point is, don't doubt me. We should never have gotten involved if we're going to be in a command structure together. Would it make you feel better if we had dinner together tonight?"

"Some."

The wind leaked slowly from my sails. The banshees fled. All the nasty names I'd been storing up to fling at her, died on my lips.

"Ok. Now pretend I kissed you passionately, since we agreed not to do that in the office and we'll meet at seven."

She turned away and was gone. Not physically, just in any locale I could reach. I gave up and left the office feeling as if I'd just lost Wheel of Fortune because I couldn't remember the phrase, 'All's Fair in Love and War.' Pardon my metaphor. I went back to my reports and began giving the contact at the ABR war desk a taste of the banshee.

JEFF - 3
Lakota Nation

Faye watched the sun through the car window. It seemed to spin above her. She'd mentioned it when we got on Highway 183 and had been mesmerized ever since. The sunlight bounced off her dazzlingly white sunglasses. She had on a 1940's movie star outfit. I always joked that she turned black and white when she wore it.

She watched the sun rotate slowly. She tried to explain the illusion. It seemed to move like a cog or a medallion, or some kind of hypnotic mandala. It was for these kinds of observations that I was elated to have her along.

Croslin had finally caved in but crustily delivered a warning. "You're uninsured though, and anything that happens to you is your own fault."

The Lakota Nation border had been extraordinarily easy to cross. The border agent didn't even have a gun. He checked our licenses and made some remark about Colorado being a pretty place, then waved us on. The landscape didn't change. Even the Highway sign for US-83 was the same except for the black splotch over the 'US.'

"What'choo lookin' at?" I used my redneck voice.

"Still looking at the sun. It stopped spinning all of the sudden." Her voice sounded dreamy and far away.

"I think you're overheated."

She began to squeal in excitement and protest. "NOOO! I'm serious. It was like it was pulling us forward along the road by an invisible rope and then that eagle flew across the sky and it stopped doing it."

"What eagle?"

"Didn't you see that big eagle fly real low over the car? It totally blocked out the sun for a couple of seconds." Faye sounded less sure of herself.

I was dumbfounded. "No I missed that..."

"Maybe I was dreaming," she mumbled. She thrashed her arm around behind the seats. "You want a granola bar or an apple or something?"

"Yeah. Gimme a granola bar."

"Whaddaya saaay?" She taunted me with the granola bar.

"Gimme a fuck-in gra-no-la bar, damn it?"

"That's better." She unwrapped it and handed it to me.

I spied a truck stop on the side of the road. "Let's stop and get some coffee."

The truck stop had obviously been a Texaco station at one time but now had no name at all. Its tacky gift shop/dining area didn't appear very different than any in the US. The clientele eyed us warily but inoffensively, the way locals and truckers always eye tourists.

I stopped inside the door and slowly turned to look at Faye. "Money."

"Didn't Croslin say they still accepted US currency?"

"At some places but I don't know about truck stops."

"Why would truck stops be the one exception. You're worrying about nothing."

She was right, I turned back around and decided to risk some coffee. Faye began goggling the horrible souvenir section, suppressing laughter at the usual display of gaudy souvenirs and trucker items. They still had spoons from nearby states, although there were none for North or South Dakota. The porcelain raccoons driving tractors that had become a craze in the last few years filled most of the top shelves. Bumper stickers of the normal trucker variety shared the shelf with fresh ones that said 'Lakota Nation' and 'The People.'

I went to the register and set my coffee down.

The checker smiled politely. "Will that be all?"

"Yeah."

"Two-oh-three."

I pulled out two US dollars and three pennies and laid them on the counter. My license slipped out and landed face up with the big Colorado flag quite visible.

The clerk quickly slammed his hand down over the license, but not before the nearest trucker caught a glimpse. The man wore a black T-shirt, with an Eagle riding a Harley-Davidson emblazoned on the chest. He had a red baseball cap that said Pfizer covering thick black hair. The lips under his Willie Nelson mustache broke into a grin.

He spoke in the redneck voice I had tried to imitate earlier. "You're not from around here, are ya."

The clerk interrupted him. "Now hold on Loony. He's got the right to be from wherever he's from. It don't mean nothin' about him."

"Don't wax legal at me Frank!"

The rational part of my brain shut down. "Your name's Loony, huh?"

The clerk's head sunk and began to shake.

Loony sneered. "Yeah, what's yours? Little Pussy Cat?"

"Strangely enough no." Faye edged up and tried to move me away. "My name is Nonuff Yourbizness."

The man lunged forward and slapped my coffee across the room. There's no excuse for slapping a man's coffee. I saw red.

"You shithead Americans think you can come back and ruin a good thing? We've got freedom here man! You're not going to pervert THIS nation the way you--"

"Yeah but people like you will."

Loony lunged for my neck but fell flat on his face as he tripped over Faye's well placed foot. He scrambled to his feet, finding himself face to face with a large man in flannel who appeared from behind me. I felt extremely small between the two men, but the sight of my coffee on the floor kept me stiff.

"The skinny one is right and very brave to say so. Maybe he keeps idiots like you from ruining things. Get outta here Loony and don't set foot near the highway. I'm sure you understand."

Loony slapped the table, grabbed his jacket and stormed out.

"Gonna send him to Rez, Eagle?"

I couldn't tell who made the crack, but laughter broke out in spots all around the truck stop.

The clerk got another cup of coffee and gave it to me, gratis.

"What's your name, man?" The tall Lakota in flannel said 'man' like he meant male human being not like 'Hey man.'

"Jeff Conroy."

"Well Jeff Conroy, from Colorado, USA, be careful in our land. We haven't yet deported all the stupid ones back to your country. We may never do it, since we have true equal rights. I'm Highway Security Marshall Craig Eagle."

"Thank you sir." I had fresh coffee. I was ready to be calm again.

"No need to sir me. I have no connection with the medieval European past. Please don't get the wrong idea about what I just did. We stick up for life. If you threaten the nation you will receive much worse treatment than Loony got."

"Why was it so easy to get in the country?" I blurted out. The break in tension had left me shaky.

"We don't believe in espionage and secrecy. Honesty is the best espionage. Our Highway Security motto is 'The ones who watch.' We all watch out for each other. Take care."

He turned and walked out to the parking lot without having changed his expression once through the entire conversation.

'Just like a cop,' I thought but then realized this man didn't strike me as a cop at all. There was no swagger or throwing weight around. He did his job and left. Actually, that's the way good cops act. I'd just run into so few of them, I'd forgot.

We climbed back in the car and pulled onto the highway. The rest of the trip to Pierre was uneventful. We had no problems checking into our motel. Familiarly road-weary, we lay down and fell to talking about Colorado and the new Montana alliance. We both worried that the situation could explode into another area war. I thought Colorado should join with Montana for its own good. Faye saw this as escalating the conflict.

"I just don't think there's any reason for Colorado to worry, unless the Aryans spread outside of Idaho."

I shook my head. "We're surrounded though. And since the Federal government isn't punishing Montana, I don't know why we don't join, just to be on the safe side. We may need the leverage against Texas, or even Utah."

"Why do we have to take a military stance on EVERYthing? There is NO reason for any of those areas to bother with Colorado. We're not that valuable."

"I don't think that matters. You're not looking at the fact that this is a greedy land grabbing game, especially for Texas. And Texas did have a small part of Colorado at one time."

"So the solution is to jump in with both feet, both fists, firing?" She jumped out of bed and began to pace.

"I know you think any military is bad military--"

"NO! That's not what I think. Don't put words in my mouth. I already told you, I understand there needs to be defense... but why... OHH Shit, look, I'm getting too riled up about this. I'm going to just go get some ice and cool off."

Faye stormed out the door and down to the ice machine.

When she tromped back, she found the screen door locked. I sat at the table inside, pretending to read a brochure. I couldn't help pulling out all the stops. I felt good getting even for the infrequent times when she got irrationally angry. I'm a stinker.

She yanked on the door a couple of times but I didn't move a muscle.

"Jeff! This isn't funny, open the goddamned door.....Jeff!"

I continued to read undisturbed.

"Jeff, Goddammit! Your juvenile little display is not proving anything except..."

I appeared at the door.

"It's very simple. You admit I'm right; I let you in."

Faye glared at me. I stared back calmly with the hint of a smile on my face. I'd already won and we both knew it. She fought for control, but her lips struggled out from under her and she began to laugh.

In-between giggles she screeched out a protest. "Dammit Jeff! Let me in."

I unlocked the door and she stormed past me.

"If you think for one minute that you are going, that I am going to be in any way amenable, to you, your... damn... right. ANYONE, ANYONE else pulls that shit and I never want to see them again."

"It doesn't work." I had absent-mindedly tried to turn on the ancient television set.

"Well, turn on the radio then and start making up for what you did."

I did.

"Another state leaves the fold out west. The Church of Jesus Christ and the Latter Day Saints declared a Mormon Nation in Utah today and negotiated a peace with California. A small part of Southwestern Wyoming also declared itself part of this Mormon Nation.

"Troubles escalated in the northwest. The Montana Coalition saw its first military action today in central Idaho against the Aryan Nation. General Andreas Melchick of the Montana National Guard remarked on the situation."

"I tell you, those guys have got a shitload of ammo and guns but they're not trained worth a damn. I give 'em six months at the outside."

"On the Arkansas front, The Ozark People's Republic pushed the Texans back into the center of the city of Little Rock. Jack Wilson has more."

With his usual backdrop of gunfire, reporter Jack Wilson bravely shouted his report.

"Thanks Greg. I'm in North Little Rock, near the McCain Mall, where Ozarkian troops have the Texans on the run. A regiment of Texan Regulars is holed up in the Mall, which the St. Louis Area Elite Unit has surrounded. I'm with Lieutenant Commander Kelly Shaw. What led to this stage Kelly?"

A tough no-nonsense woman's voice began talking in an Arkansas accent.

"Well, after a lightning raid down McCain Boulevard by the Southern Illinois Boys, we had a clear drive for the St. Louis boys to break off on each side and hound out the Texans, which is what we're finishing up here. After that, we unleashed the Missouri and Arkansas Ozark Specials, which pushed the surprised Texans down over the river and into downtown, where they're holding the line for the moment."

"How hard is it going to be to cross the Arkansas River?"

"Well, Caesar got across the Rubicon and Washington made the Delaware and I think the Ozarkians'll soon be wavin' the Texans goodbye 'cross the Texarkana line."

"That's big talk." You could hear Jack smile.

"And we can back it up."

"Lieutenant Kelly Shaw, of the Ozark People's Army. Back to you Greg."

"Ozark troops also appeared in Kansas City. Spokespersons said they are merely recruiting.

"Fearing the Texans, the Ozarkians and the Lakota Nation, a collection of state governments in the center of the US announced the formation of the Great Plains Alliance. The Alliance will work, in their words 'to preserve and defend the states abandoned by the United States military.' Nebraska, Kansas and the South Dakota government in Sioux City, make up the coalition. Spokespersons described it as a temporary coalition, with a central military command but no central government.

"This is American Belief Radio in New York. I'm Greg Whitney."

KOLBRASKI - 4
Texas Military Prison

The fluorescent lights in the holding room could hardly be called light. They didn't illuminate so much as cause everything to glow as if slightly spoiled. Four Texas Military Policemen played cards under a banker's lamp which shed just enough real light to see the betting. Another MP sat squinting at a magazine, which seemed to have lost its color. The only guard presently acting as if on duty, walked over to the cheap Deskset near the door and shut off the netcast. He turned and faced the row of county jail cells holding the prisoners of war. 50 men and women crammed into 15 cells.

A loud MP stomped past the cells. "Lights out y'all.

I slumped back on my cot and looked at John. We'd been through a lot together. So much didn't need to be spoken, even now.

"Well, Mcgillicutty. I guess you were right. We shouldn't have been in the same unit."

"Listen Kolby," he said gently, "Gehrig will get us out. Just sit tight," he held up a hand, "I know what you're thinking but cut it out. You heard the radio..."

"The press, John, I don't--"

"The details don't matter. We're well into Little Rock, once we get there, negotiations can begin."

I sighed. John didn't realize Gehrig hadn't been trained in emergency unit recall. IF he got back to HQ, it would be a miracle if he remembered enough details to give Intelligence any kind of useful lead. I couldn't remember much myself after hitting the wall. We'd woke in the back of some truck with several other Ozarkians and a few random looters. I looked at the linoleum that lined the floor and walls of the cell, still gleaming in the darkness somehow. I felt imprisoned in a country kitchen. I almost mentioned this to John but, then, he always sort of liked the country kitchen stuff.

Suddenly, the lights went back on.

"Awright, Kolbraski, McGill, this is your new commanding officer Captain Anne Bartholomew. Welcome to the proud Texas Shock Fighters 55th."

Two MP's yanked us out of our bed and marched us down the hall. We approached a door and Captain Bartholomew slapped blindfolds on us.

The MPs pushed us out into the night air, up some steps and into soft cushioned seats. I heard many other people muttering around us.

"Kolby?"

"Yeah," I grunted, confirming my presence. I felt his hand touch mine briefly.

A voice like bricks flying through a window pierced through the darkness. "Quiet for the Captain!"

Captain Bartholomew's thinner but more confident voice, rose with the pitch of an engine, which I guessed to be a jet.

"Yew, Ladies and Gentlemen, are on Flight 136 to El Paso via San Antonio. You have been selected as fine fighting troops to serve in the Texas Shock Fighters 55th. You WILL obey orders or receive punishment. Baader!"

"Yes."

"I'm afraid, Baader, that the response in this unit is yes Captain, Lieutenant, administer."

I heard grunts and groans and several whacks.

"From now on, however, the unit will be punished as a whole for infractions of any sort. Punishment will be delivered in a timely matter, by the fine Lieutenants in this unit who outnumber you 2 to 1. As soon as we reach cruising altitude we will unblindfold and uncuff you. Please relax for the flight to Dallas."

I doubted the 2 to 1 ratio. Especially since the Lieutenants were all squeezed in the first class cabin. When the blindfolds were released, I began to talk to John, wary of the Lieutenant monitoring all conversations. We spoke in the TV code we'd developed in college. John agreed the Flintstones couldn't beat the Jetsons. We arrived in Dallas and sat on the ground.

What must have been several hours, dragged by without relief. The Lieutenants gave us hard bagels for lunch. Still speaking in TV code, John and I decided they probably lied about El Paso and that when we got to wherever we were going, we would try what the Ozarkians call a dual escape. From there, we would try to head north. The Lieutenants monitoring the conversation heard an argument over whether M*A*S*H, Cheers or Friends had the best final episode of the 20th Century.

STEVE - 8
Dallas, Texas

Helen and I drove north on highway 35E. We had packed the things we couldn't leave behind and the rest would just have to stay. We couldn't take much because we didn't want to look like we were going anywhere permanently. We headed through Dallas on our way to Denton to see Mulu. I hoped Mulu had a plan to get us to Oklahoma City, where we could sneak along Oklahoma 66 into Missouri.

As we came off a bridge, north of Dallas, flashing lights appeared in my rear view mirror. I pulled the car over.

"Listen, Helen, don't worry. We're just headed to Denton to visit Mulu, that's all."

The policeman approached the car and leaned down to the window.

"Mornin' sir." I gushed pleasantness to cover my nerves.

"May I see your license please?"

"Of course, sir, what's the problem?"

The policeman took the license and radioed the number into headquarters.

"Sir, you weren't doing anything wrong and you're free to travel about as you please but we have had some escaped prisoners from the Arkansas terrorist groups operating in these parts. Do you mind if I ask where you're headed?"

"Up to Denton to see a friend."

The radio crackled with some unintelligible reports.

"You're free to go sir, but be careful in Denton. We've had some trouble there recently. Have a nice day."

"What did he mean by trouble?" Helen meant it as a statement.

"I don't know, but I'm sure the police are wholly innocent."

"What do you mean?" Helen looked at me horrified.

"I was being sarcastic," I snapped.

"Oh, well you don't have to get mad."

"I'm sorry, the cops always make me nervous. You know that."

"I know." She reached over and touched my hand looking at me tentatively. I didn't want to smile but I did and so did she. And suddenly everything was fine for Helen. It's like the whole thing never happened because I smiled.

When we arrived at Mulu's house no one was there. I found an envelope on the porch. It was written in Russian, which I translated for

Helen.

"Hello Steve and Helen. I must fly to Big Bend. You should join me. There are two tickets in the envelope. See you there."

The tickets were for flights to El Paso.

"Whaddaya think?" I waved the tickets.

Helen looked puzzled. "Is he trying to tell us something?"

"Yeah, I think so. And that policeman wasn't happy about us going north towards Oklahoma. We'd probably get turned back if we went. What's to lose?"

"All we have now is Mulu. We have to follow him."

There were very few security checks as we got on the plane to El Paso. No one was trying to leave Texas or enter Texas through El Paso. However, when we disembarked, there were several security checks, which puzzled me. Why the sudden interest after we'd already gotten here. Something new was definitely being brewed up by Governor Morgan. Every day the Texans surprised me. I couldn't wait to get back to a normal government and stable existence. Goddamn the Texans. After marching down an aisle lined on one side with Texan military troops, we found Mulu in the main gateway area, near a packed security station.

Helen ran up and hugged him.

I almost did too. "We are really glad to see you."

"Yeah." Helen looked the most enthusiastic I'd seen her in months.

"I'm terribly glad y'all took my offer. There's a somewhat secret security sweep going on north of Denton. If you'd gotten pulled over, you might've been fine, Steve, but Helen would've been carted off to who knows where. Anyone without a Texas citizenship paper or license is mysteriously disappearing."

"We have a car?" Helen looked surprised.

"Yeah and we're going to Big Bend where a friend of mine and yours will see to it we have a great time." Mulu had a strange look in his eyes. He peered down at his watch and pressed a couple of buttons. It looked like he was checking the date or setting an alarm. I knew better. "Yeah, let's get going."

At the rental office, Mulu presented an investigator's badge and a fake Texas passport/diplomatic ID. This sped up the now lengthy paperwork in Texas for renting a car, and allowed us to get an 'unrestricted' car. Most cars had the new Texas Republic plates with the Lone Star hologram behind the number. The hologram allowed police to check background on the driver. Unrestricted cars had the old plain black and white plates that had no hologram and read, 'Texas Exempt.'

Before getting in the car, Mulu opened his small suitcase and pulled out something that looked like an air freshener.

He grinned at me again, in a slightly disconcerting manner.

"I hate the smell of these rental cars. You never know who's been in them."

He sprayed the interior of the car, while staring at the can intently. He motioned for us to get in and when we were out of sight of the rental office he pulled something out of his watch and placed it under the visor of the car.

"Ok. Now we can talk. That's a small scrambler I worked up, in case anyone's eavesdropping on us. My watch scans for minute resonating waves put out by most pick-up mikes. That airport was heavily bugged. I doubt they've got a scope on this car but you never know. If they do, now they'll get a slight buzz and radio noise, with me going on for three hours about how great Big Bend is and how I love Texas."

I looked at Mulu with my usual sense of wonder and admiration. "What was in that spray can?"

"Here." Mulu handed the can to me. "Press the spray nozzle and look closely at the logo."

As I did so a faint holographic image formed over the logo. An incomprehensible set of symbols and numbers played out across the surface. Rapidly switching back and forth.

"It scans a ten foot area for bugs and other monitoring devices that may be implanted in the car. I was extremely surprised to find an official car without them. El Paso's more backwater than I thought."

I put the can on the floorboard. "Aren't you a little paranoid?"

"He's just careful." Helen leaned forward into the front seat grinning.

"You can't be too careful in this Republic." Mulu nodded.

He took Route-54 out of El Paso and into the Fort Bliss Military Reservation. He explained it was less conspicuous to drive an official car through the little used reservation, than past the checkpoint on I-10.

"Since secession, the reservation has been split between New Mexico and Texas anyway, so no one's really sure what's going on outside of El Paso."

After taking a gravel side road that went harrowingly through the Organ Mountains, Mulu stopped the car. He pulled a New Mexico 'Veteran' plate out of his suitcase and removed the Texas plates. A mile down the road we came upon US-70.

"We are now in the undisputed territory of the United States of America again," he said.

All I could see was an empty road and dust. I asked Mulu why we didn't encounter a border check.

"I don't know, actually. They have a border check on the eastern and northern border of New Mexico. They practically consider it part of Texas. Maybe that's why they don't patrol the southern border. Still, we can make it to Las Cruces and hide with the friends I told you would be in Big Bend."

"Do you really think they were spying on us enough, that you had to lie about Big Bend?"

"I don't know. I don't think they're out following us with helicopters but they might have tried, if we'd spilled all the beans."

Helen leaned forward. "So we're going to stay with Simone and Sam?"

Mulu answered before I could. "Yeah. I mailed them and we surreptitiously worked out a plan. She caught on pretty quick that I was talking about coming there, instead of meeting in Big Bend."

Helen said nothing more about staying with Simone but I knew it bothered her. I wanted to say something but nothing seemed appropriate. There really was nothing between Simone and me.... Anymore.

I turned to Helen. "It's cool if we stay with Sam and Simone?"

She laughed shortly. "Where else are we gonna go? Yeah, it's fine."

I left it at that. I hoped it stayed there.

Thirty minutes later, in Las Cruces, we pulled up to a small low wooden house with a big yard. An elk hound bounded up to the fence behind and began to bark.

"Manik! Quiet!" A man dressed in a white button up shirt and black jeans bounded down the porch towards us.

Mulu took the lead as usual. "Hey Sam, what's cookin'?"

"Just makin' some salmon, come on in." He grabbed Helen's bag and led the way back into the house.

The house was dark and cinnamony. Helen and I sank down on the couch while Mulu followed Sam into the pink kitchen.

I knew the whole idea of seeing Simone again made Helen upset. I started to say something and so did Helen.

"Oh I'm sorry," Helen squeaked.

"Nothing, what were you going to say?"

"Well, what's the plan now? Are all of us going west?"

"I think so. Mulu wants it to seem like a friendly little vacation instead of a fugitive rush."

Just then the door opened.

"Hi-i," Simone's eyes caught mine. "Oh, hey! You guys made it."

She set the groceries down and gave me a big hug. "So how was your trip?" She looked at Helen then back at me.

"Fine. Hey, thanks for doin' this."

"No problem. I'm there for you man." She gave a little smile and hurried off into the kitchen.

Sam came back out. "Anyone for salmon?"

"Sure!" Helen yelled quickly and loudly.

Sam graciously served and we graciously ate.

After several minutes of wolfing down food, Mulu began pontificating on the Texas situation. "They're not going to open another front. I think they may try to get New Mexico to join them like Western Louisiana and Oklahoma, but they're not going to invade."

"Nah, they're going to grab as much as they can WHILE they can," I replied. "They'll make an excuse in New Mexico and they've already got one in Louisiana. They've got to expand they're borders to keep them safe. As long as they know the iron's hot, they're going to strike it over and over again. They have to."

Sam shook his head. "I don't know Yogi. I think that might be a bit stupid even for the Texans. I mean, wars cost money. And all of the states are broke. There's no way they could afford it."

Mulu considered Sam's words. "Hmmm. I don't know... well, take this as second hand hearsay but a friend of mine mailed me a part of a UN report which supposedly showed German Euros being funneled into Texan banks and Italian Euros being deposited in banks all over California."

Simone stood up. "I don't like conspiracy theories very much but I've seen some pretty strange 'German' tourists come through the Book Store, all on their way to El Paso. I'm gonna go have a cigarette."

I jumped up. "Me too."

"Steve!" Helen cried.

"Oh come on, one isn't gonna kill me. Besides, I've had a very stressful day. I'll be right back. Don't worry."

Simone sat on the porch looking off down the street. She turned to me. "I miss you like fuck."

I touched her arm. "Yeah, I miss you too."

"How are things?"

"Ok," I murmured.

"She forgiven you yet?"

"I don't know."

"Of course not and she won't. Idiot."

"Don't talk about her like that."

"I'm sorry. She just makes me so mad because she makes you unhappy."

"I'm not unhappy now. I'm just not happy."

"Yeah, and that's not right."

I stared straight out into the sandy field of scrub. "Maybe it's not, but now when everything is falling apart I've got to hold what little of my life there is together. It's like Texas starting all those wars for self-preservation. Is that too pretentious?"

"No, just overly dramatic. Your life isn't that bad. It could be... I don't know..."

"You happy?" I turned her honesty back on her.

"Oh yeah. Sammy's great. Everything I could want. I still get restless though. Wondering. You know."

"You're in the same position as me, Simone. Always have been. When will we ever learn?"

"We won't. We better get back inside, before they start inventing new scandals about us."

Mulu and Sam were arguing about whether import beers or impoverished war refugees, were more important on incoming cargo ships.

Sam valiantly defended the beer. "And finally, even the finest brewed refugee is not drinkable," he finished.

Helen sat punching buttons on a sofamote. "Your TV doesn't work."

Simone looked neutrally at Helen. "No, it doesn't. I'm sorry. Hasn't worked in months and they're hard to find parts for now. Do you want to listen to the netcast?" Her gaze briefly rested on Sam and then settled pleasantly on me.

I answered without thinking. "Sure."

"This is the week in review on American Belief Radio. We stand for unity."

"American Belief Radio's week in review. I'm Jerry Martinez.

"Chicago and Detroit formed a new nation this week. They claimed a thin swath of land in Northern Indiana and Southern Michigan, placing armed guards along Interstates 90 and 94. African-American Front gunmen required all passengers on the highway to pay an increased toll. George Halberstam has more."

"Commuters outside Chicago were annoyed by the delay getting on the East West Toll Road outside Gary. But beyond that, many weren't too concerned about the change in government."

A refined Chicago accent spoke over the noise of traffic.

"Well I don't like the toll but nobody does, so whaddaya gonna do?"

George asked a question from off-mike. "Are you worried about the African-American Front taking over Chicago and Detroit?"

"I'm shoor they'll do a helluva lot better than the Democrats but, uh, you know, party's change but everything always stays the same."

"Well what about the secession?"

"I gotta get to work."

A new more earthy Belmont voice began to speak.

"They what? Goddamn it. They better not, uh, shut down Fairmont."

Another, younger voice took over.

"So are the Bears leavin' town then?"

George Halberstam returned with his accent-free, studio-modulated voice.

"The Windy City seems to be riding this one out fairly obliviously. Jerry?"

"Thanks George. Talks have begun in St. Louis among Minnesota, Illinois, Wisconsin, Missouri, and Ohio about defending against the alliance in Chicago.

"The Ozarkians finally pushed the Texans out of Little Rock. ABR lost one of our best reporters in the battle. Jack Wilson's greatest dream was to cover a peace conference which would end the fighting. All of us here will miss Jack greatly.

"After freeing Little Rock, the Ozarkians began massing troops in Kansas City and along the border of Memphis.

"Texas is manning the Colorado border. The President has advised Colorado to prepare its militia to join the US Army against a Texan attack. Colorado governor Wilson Gregory remarked, 'What US Army?'

"And the governors of Tennessee and Kentucky, met to discuss their states' positions should the Midwestern states ally. The two states feel threatened by the Ozark People's Republic."

"Jack Wilson died!?" My mouth gaped.

"Yeah, I heard the report." Simone spoke in monotone, looking at the floor. "He was in mid-sentence and there was this big explosion and then that Lieutenant from the Ozarks picked up the mike and said Jack was hurt."

"Oh my God." Helen's eyes widened and she drew her hand to her mouth. "The world is such an awful place. Why do we always have to hear about it."

"There are a lot more people than him dead." Mulu also stared at the ground. "He's just the most apparent in our lives 'cause he's so well known."

We all looked at one another silently. A wind picked up and whistled through the cracks of the house and out into the New Mexico desert.

JEFF - 4
Cheyenne Reservation, Lakota Nation

The wind whipped through the 12 acre stretch of what used to be the Cheyenne River Indian Reservation near Eagle Butte, the Lakota had just completed the first three buildings in what was to be a 12 building complex. I noticed immediately upon arrival, how different the place looked from most institutional buildings in the US. The harsh badlands burst forth with green and flowers in the land around the compound. Inmates worked tending the plants here and there. The administration worked in a low green building made of glowing metal and glass. It blended into the lush landscape like a green-backed beetle. The main work-hall looked something like a castle without turrets, made of adobe. Inside, inmates attended classes, or created mostly practical arts and crafts. The third building, the first of the residence housing, resembled an old log cabin with chimneys on either end. Inside, the modern attributes of stainless steel and electrical outlets, blended seamlessly with the wood and earth interior.

It was one of the most informative stops we had made so far. Croslin had gone crazy over what I'd already sent back but I knew it was nothing compared to what I'd shot today.

After touring the compound and then several of its many nature walks and gardening preserves, we stood, relaxed, in front of the Administration building under the shade of a large oak tree.

Faye looked back over the path that led amongst the compound buildings. Men worked at different projects with an air of ease. "So the reservations are pretty much just halfway houses?"

"Well, yes and no." White Deer eagerly began to explain. He seemed to derive great pleasure from detailing the finer points of the Lakota's governing philosophy. "For many, it is halfway to nowhere. Those unfortunate people drain the spirit, and our budget. Many we will try to convince to leave for the US. Some few will be deported for actual crimes. No one who really wants to stay in Lakota Nation and who lived here before the liberation, will be forced to leave. We know that lesson too well."

Jeff took another shot of the 'inmates' working in the community garden. He looked up at White Deer. Their guide had led them around the reservation for two hours, patiently, even enthusiastically, answering all manner of questions. All officials of Lakota Nation shared White

Deer's enthusiasm. There were no evasions and rarely were questions refused. It got kind of weird, you know, having them always telling you everything like that. I wanted to catch them hiding something.

White Deer was an affable, intense man, thin but muscular, about the same height as me. He had long black hair, sky blue eyes and wore the olive green uniform of a reservation attendant.

The only time he'd disrupted his calm manner, was at the site of the old settlement at Eagle Butte. He spoke of the horrible conditions the Sioux had lived in.

"Like Pigs." A dark look steeled his blue eyes to gray. "It was to end this and never have another Lakota, or Human Being, ever be treated like that again, that the Lakota Nation arose."

The rundown shacks and 'houses' were preserved there, some with the junk and paltry possessions left intact as a reminder of what was, now, in the past for the Lakota.

Now back in the present, White Deer smiled and seemed as much a part of the surroundings as the garden.

I took one last shot. "Well I think that about does it, thanks for your help. You've been extremely patient."

"It's no problem. I know what you mean, but most of us in Lakota Nation see the importance and even pleasure, in explaining our country to others, especially those with open minds. In some ways we consider it a duty. We hope the world can follow our lead and loose the Earth, including humanity, from its bonds."

We said goodbye and White Deer invited us back to Cheyenne Rez any time. We climbed in the rental car and headed down LNH-14 to Pierre. There was a good hour and a half of driving ahead of us and we had to catch a plane, early the next morning.

Faye chomped into an apple with gusto. Some of White Deer's enthusiasm had rubbed off. "That guard was aMAZing. What a wonderful individual. I wanted to invite him home or something. He was just great."

"Yeah, he certainly was."

"I mean, this Nation is so incredible. Jeff, your story is so much more important than anyone realizes. I mean, this could be a model utopia in a way. I mean, I'm not saying everything here is perfect but they're so AWARE of what's going on. You know what I mean?"

"Yeah."

"What's wrong?"

"This heat gauge keeps heading up towards hot and then falling back. It's probably nothing but it's sort of unnerving. Sorry. Go ahead."

"No that's all right. If you need to concentrate, I don't want to--"

Suddenly, a loud pop came from the front of the car and steam rolled out from under the hood. I let off the accelerator quickly. "I don't think that's good."

Faye agreed, and we rolled to the side of the road.

"Should we even try popping the hood?"

"Well, if we wait for this steam to roll off, it'll probably be fine. If the hood's not too hot."

When the steam died down, I popped the hood and Faye gingerly raised it.

The engine sizzled and steamed.

I stared at it. "It's broke."

Faye stared just as helplessly. "Nutters."

A Highway Patrol car pulled up and Security Marshall Eagle got out.

"Jeff Conroy. I see you have a problem with that fine American Car. Can I help?"

I laughed and shook hands with the Marshall. "Well, we can't send it back to Detroit. They seceded, you know. What do we do with this fine piece of American Engineering now that there isn't much USA left?"

"Well, that car's the property of a business in the State of Colorado, which means I can't legally touch it. However, I can give you a ride back to Pierre, where you can contact a mechanic to come get it. The tow'll be.... Do you have AAA?"

I laughed again. "You sound as if all fifty are just happily living together."

"Triple A is a multinational organization. More so today. It still works here."

Faye came around from the front of the car grinning. "Yes, we have Triple A."

"Ok. So the tow will be free and then you can decide what you want to do with the car."

The inside of the Security car was unlike any police vehicle I had ever seen. There were no mounds of sophisticated equipment or barriers or cages or anything.

I found one missing piece of equipment especially surprising. "Don't you have a radar gun?"

"No. We do have speed limits, but the spirit of the law is to avoid recklessness. If I see someone driving recklessly, I pull them over, no matter what speed they are going. You see, speeding is not a money making device for us. Some people receive other punishments, besides fines, for reckless driving. Any fines that are levied, go to the Highway Safety Association, which educates the public. None of it goes to the Department of Security, or the state."

Faye read my thoughts. "What were you doing out here? I don't mean to be rude but it's an incredible coincidence."

"No. I was not following you." Eagle grinned slightly.

"I didn't think you were." Faye turned slightly red.

Eagle paused. "No, I do not think you did. You two are good people. I don't say those words often. I was doing a security check on the area outside the Rez. No one has left the Rez without clearance but it's a standard check to see if anyone has lost their way."

We talked non-politically most of the rest of the way back to Pierre. Eagle told us about his wife and two daughters. I told him about the University and Faye delighted him with tales from the animal shelter. He fascinated me with his ability to talk evenly on almost any subject whatsoever. I decided to push it a little as I am always too quick to do. Here was my chance to bring a little light on any sort of dark underbelly the Lakota might have.

"There has to be something wrong with the Lakota Nation, Marshall. I mean, everyone talks so glowingly and reasonably about how everything works so smoothly. Honestly, It's a little creepy."

At first, the Marshall seemed stumped, then I noticed him grinning. "You cannot start the fire by asking the log to light, Jeff. You have not seen all there is to see. However, did you not meet Loony on the first day you arrived?"

"Yeah."

"And in your studies, have you never read of the good Chief, or King, surrounded with bad advisers?"

"Ok. Sure."

"What makes you think we're so different?"

"But everyone involved with the Nation seems to be so well-intentioned and well-adjusted."

"They have seen their battles and want to make a peace now. Make it work. That takes cooperation. We hope to get it by not forcing it."

"But then, you might not get it."

"Of course not. But our eyes are open. Unlike the US lawmakers, we do not shut our senses off and speak. We keep quiet and watch."

"What do you do if the whites get tired of this in a couple of years and try to take over the government? Or to make it non-racial, what if a bunch of creeps get into office?"

"We have spent centuries waiting. A few years is not large enough to see, nor small enough to handle."

I gave up. "Are you sure you're not a Zen master instead of a highway Marshall."

Eagle laughed. "You see without knowing, sometimes. Zen is very important in our studies, Jeff. Though not as important as the old ways." He laughed again. It filled the car with music.

When we got back to the hotel, Eagle stopped us outside the car. He pulled two feathers from his shirt pocket and placed one in each of our palms. "You are welcome to visit my tribe in any season. Do not feel obligated to say anything. They are feathers. Merely a token I give to friends."

"Thank you, Eagle. You are more than welcome to come visit us in Colorado anytime," I replied awkwardly.

Faye nodded her agreement.

"If my journeys take me there, I will be sure to look you up." He smiled and waved goodbye as we walked slowly back to the hotel room.

Faye looked enraptured by the feathers. "That was so cool."

"Yeah."

We called Croslin, who sounded uncharacteristically nervous. He told us to forget the car and get a plane back to Denver as soon as possible.

"Look, I'm not making any predictions, but it'd be safer for you to get back here. If the Texans do take Denver, you'll lose everything; possessions, bank accounts, everything. If you get back soon, you'll have time to consolidate all that. The State is helping people wonderfully."

I hung up and explained the situation to Faye.

She looked uncharacteristically worried. "That's worse than I thought. I didn't think the Texans were that close."

"Yeah, we better go. I still don't like the idea of ditching the car."

"Let's sell it." Faye looked at me stone faced.

I caught the corner of her mouth start to rise for just a second. I lunged at her but she stepped out of the way and threw me on the bed.

"That's the last time you try that with me mithter," she jumped on me.

The noise scared off a hawk owl outside our hotel window. It flew straight up across the moon and disappeared.

KANDEL - 3
Tucson, Arizona

I sat in the diner, half-listening and staring out the window. An owl had landed in the gravel outside and was picking at some breadcrumbs in the rocks. My thoughts pecked along with the owl. Why would Stephanie put the fate of two whole states in the undersecretary's hands? This was ridiculous. I mean, I knew I could do the job but this was important stuff. Not two-bit phone calls to two-bit news editors, to give them a four-bit work over. Shit, if I failed, it could be in part because I lacked credibility. I mean I WAS only the Undersecretary. Why did she want me away from Nevada so badly? She wasn't that cowardly. Was she? I knew the answer. I just didn't want to even think it. Coward. I knew I better not be a coward when it came to the negotiations, which I suddenly realized I hadn't been paying any attention to. I stopped chewing and looked at the Apache Chief.

"I mean it." The Chief looked at me wild eyed, for what reason, I hadn't a clue. He seemed to go on and on about nothing anyway. Who could tell what it was this time. Wait, that wasn't fair. He was just what you call passionate and I was just, what you call, depressed.

"With the number of Apache in Arizona and New Mexico, there is no way and no reason we should not be independent." He grimaced for emphasis and shook his head.

"I don't doubt you." I put on my most diplomatic, 'I've been called on by the teacher and have no idea what's going on,' voice. "It's just that the Texas Army is going strong now, and the Lakota didn't have to face anything like that." That was good. An important point I'd tried to get across, I don't know, a million times, and applicable to just about anything he could've been going on about.

"And what would you suggest, UNDERsecretary Kandel?"

Ow! That hurt. I stayed calm and imagined myself to be Chamberlain talking to Hitler. No! Strike that. Not a good analogy. How about somebody who won? None of the diplomats ever won. Just the crazy monsters. Ok, what the hell, Ben Franklin was a bit of a rogue and talked a blue streak with the French.

"A political takeover of each state. You could use Peace Party apparatus but you wouldn't have to. I think with a little more work, you could do it on your own AND you wouldn't risk armed intervention from Texas, which, as I have made clear, will provoke armed intervention from California."

"Waiting for political takeover would mean waiting until the US is strong enough to stop us. Besides, Texas will invade anyway, whether we revolt or not."

"You can speed up political reform, especially if you use Peace Party methods and with a California alliance to protect you," I struck the table emphatically. "Texas will NOT attack."

"No thank you. The lesser of two evils IS California. But our Apache confederation will stand on its own feet. Not two feet but two million feet." He made a grand wide-eyed gesture.

I slumped back in my chair. Ding! Round 10 and match, or something like that. My last attempt to avoid war had obviously failed. I couldn't even eat. But I could drink. "More coffee please."

It was no wonder I couldn't forge peace. We were eating at Denny's. We talked about other things and after two more cups of coffee, I stood up jaggedly feeling the caffeine binding tightly to my neurons. I laid a 50 US dollar bill on the table. Nice things, those expense accounts.

"That'll only cover the coffee." The Apache Chief's eyes crinkled in laughter.

I smiled and shook hands with the Chief.

"I'm still against your plans but since you won't be moved, I hope you're right and I'm wrong." What a guy I was. Now I felt like Chamberlain.

The Chief nodded and the group broke up.

I drove back to the Arizona Peace Party office on Congress St., and called Stephanie in L.A., to tell her the revolt was still on for the next day.

"Ok then." Her thin voice seemed far away and less than caring. "You're to hand over command to Commodore Vasquez and take up a cultural post."

"Aren't you coming down?"

"No. I've got a deskload of domestic affairs to handle and Carson City still isn't wrapped."

"You can't take a short reconnaissance trip... or you don't want to?" I was bouncing around inside my rib cage with coffee jitters.

"Look, Mark, I want to see you too, but until things calm down, our personal life..."

"Yeah, I know and I'm the best one for the job. Bullshit and you know it. Why don't you want to come down here?"

"We'll talk when you've calmed down, Mark."

"No. Listen, Steph--" I heard the click at the other end. I hate that click. Nothing sends me off like two pots of bad coffee and that click. I put the phone gently back in the cradle and saw her picture on the desk. Suddenly it flew through the air and hit with a crash of shattering glass, followed by several other objects large and small, clattering against the walls of the office. I hadn't really contemplated throwing a temper tantrum but once I was into it, it seemed like a good idea.

I sputtered to a halt, out of breath, but the noise of falling objects continued. I thought maybe I'd started another angry fit without knowing it but then I noticed cries and shouts adding to the clatter. I'd caused quite a ruckus. I knew Tucson was sort of a quiet town but can't a guy throw a fit in his own office without getting stormed by disturbed villagers. I opened the dirty window expecting to see a nineteenth century lynch mob, with burning torches and a signed noise complaint. I was much more surprised to hear clattering gunshots. I ducked to one side and saw undefined figures moving through the streets.

A police car raced down Congress St. and suddenly, almost magically, flipped over and exploded into flames as five men ran out to manage the wreckage. I felt like I was watching a bad action film and then it sunk in that the revolt had started early and I had to get Vasquez on the scene and order the California Militia into Tucson before the Texans.

I quickly dialed the Tucson California Peace Party office. "Get me Commodore Vasquez," I barked. It's not like me to bark but gunshots unnerve me.

There was an unseemly pause. I thanked my stars there was no hold music. Finally, a voice returned.

"Commodore Vasquez has been rushed to University Medical with a gunshot wound, Mr. Kandel. We're waiting for orders from Blythe."

I hung up and called Field General Reynolds in Blythe.

"Mike. This is Kandel in Tucson. You've got a shot up Commodore and an office full of bureaucrats sitting around here, while the city it doth burn."

"Well Mark, I guess that means you're in charge. Get that unit together and either secure city hall or make some sort of cooperative arrangement with the Apaches, whichever you think is best. We'll have reinforcements there in two hours."

I ran out the door to get over to the CPP office. As I headed downstairs, I ran into, no literally ran, as in running, into, as in physically buffeting, the Apache Chief. He bounced off me and continued lurching slowly up the stairs. His eyes were wide open, with pupils as big as eight balls. I was about to scream at him about starting the riots early, when I noticed blood racing down the side of his face.

He stumbled up one more step, spun like a doll and landed in an awkward position against the railing.

I kneeled at his side.

"Can you talk?"

A low throat clearing emptied out of the man's pale lips.

"Early.... I knew but... risked meeting.... Very wrong."

"Don't try to speak." I tried to ease the Apache chief into a sitting position. Now up close, I could see the blood on his head wasn't the worst of his worries. He had a dark splotch on his vest that wasn't Denny's catsup. I noticed three small tears in the vest, dangerously near the heart.

"I want to tell you." The Chief began to wheeze again. "You are brave... and... strong. We will cooperate. My son... Mike.... He must be safe."

A coughing fit racked the Chief. I heard footsteps coming up the stairs, just when I didn't want them. I tried to move the Chief but had no time. A dark-haired man in Apache clothing came around the bend in the stairs and shot twice at the Apache Chief before he had hardly looked at him. The bullets whistled past my left leg, grazing my instep in a blinding burn.

"Who are you?" The man pointed the gun at me.

Before I had a chance to speak, he fell down clutching his arm. I turned around and saw three Apaches with army rifles pointing past him.

"Good question," snapped a short man with sandy-brown hair, who stood in the middle of the group.

"I'm undersecretary Mark Kandel of the California Peace Party." I involuntarily raised my hands. I rarely had guns pulled on me and never without my wallet changing hands. I doubt they were interested in that.

"I am Mike Wind. That was my Father you were trying to save. I am honored by your effort. I have no time to go into detail but immediately after the revolt started, a faction of the Apache Nation, called Purity, began to riot and demand the ouster of my Father as Chief. They didn't like him cooperating with the CPP, even a small amount. I am the new Chief now. I'll cooperate as much as is fair. We need the CPP now, because the Texans will attack. Who's in command of the California Militia? Some Vasquez or someone?"

"Yeah. Could you put the guns down? Thanks. I've had a lot of coffee today. Vasquez was shot and the CM is on their way from Blythe.

So, until they get here, I'm in charge. I need to get to CPP headquarters. Now."

"We'll take you and set up a joint operation there. The California Militia will be allowed to operate in this area as long as they don't interfere. They are welcome to help. I don't want a joint command but I want our two organizations near to each other, in case of miscommunication."

Suddenly, Mike Wind looked at his Father as if trying to remember something. The glimmer of a tear appeared in the corner of one eye.

"Mark, will you do me the honor of helping me carry my Father to the car."

"Yeah. I mean, yes of course."

Mike Wind closed his father's eyes and began removing several things from his pockets.

GEHRIG - 2
St. Louis, Missouri

I walked swiftly down a dark corridor. People whispered behind doors but I couldn't find the doors. Every time I stopped to find the whisperings,a wind stirred up and nausea welled up in my chest. I had to keep walking to get away from the wind. As I walked, I tried hard to catch the whispers. 'Apple,' 'delicate,' 'stable,' and 'porcupine,' were all I managed to make out.

Occasionally, the corridor twisted and turned and the darkness would lighten to gray. Then it twisted again and I fell back into blackness. I had the overwhelming sense that if I could just remember some key thing, I could find my way out of this labyrinth. I felt like I was taking a life or death test, which I definitely hadn't studied for. After what seemed like days of walking, the gray began to lighten even more. My steps felt more sure and familiar. I gained confidence, as the whispering sounds receded and the corridors became white. Other sounds began to replace the whisperings. The light became blinding but I knew I was on the right track. Now the brightness blinded me as much as the darkness. Instead of walking, I felt like I was floating on a soft bed of air. I felt a strange sensation in my face, around the eyes and the whiteness intensified. A form lurked close to me on the right and said something unintelligible.

I heard sounds of machinery and the whiteness faded and dissolved into a fluorescent light. The figure loomed over me again. This time I understood the words.

"Can you hear me Rob?"

I tried to speak but my mouth had been on a two-week cruise and had forgotten how to move. I nodded my head instead.

"Good. If you can, try to speak. But don't push yourself."

I gave it another shot and managed the word 'spooky' which came out "boogee."

"Good Rob," the form said, unperturbed by the enigmatic word.

The old routine started to come back to my mouth and I muttered, "Whirr emeye?"

"Well Rob, you're at Barnes Hospital in St. Louis, Missouri."

"Whad happened?" I slurred.

"If you can, why don't you tell me as much as you remember." The form resolved itself into a 5' 6" woman with short blonde hair and a stethoscope.

"Who are you?"

"I'm Doctor Katrinov."

I began to tell her about the corridors and the whispering but the memory of it seemed to dissipate as I recalled it. "But before that, I was driving a car in Little Rock. I don't know how much I can tell you 'bout it."

"I assure you, it's fine to tell me everything. St. Louis is in close cooperation with the Ozarkians. Here's my badge."

She showed me an Ozarkian ID, which listed her as Dr. Lyuba Katrinov M.D., O.P.C., Medic, First Class.

"I was driving a car," I continued, "and this tank came up and Kolbraski was looking at me funny and I was all smiling and the next thing I know... well I don't know anything after that. It just sort of ends."

Dr. Katrinov moved her hands over me while she spoke. "You drove into a brick wall. Your buddies all scattered out of the car and two of them, uh, John Mcgillicutty and Mack Kolbraski were captured by the Texans. Being knocked out cold kept you from being caught. The Ozarkians finally pushed the Texans out of that area and you were found in a coma. They flew you here on your parent's wishes, rather than treat you somewhere in Little Rock or Memphis. We couldn't detect any brain damage but you've been out cold for days."

"Yeah. I was having this weird dream. Man. So, what happened to John and Kolbraski? Did they get out?"

"No Rob. I have some bad news for you about the whole squad. Are you ok?"

"Yeah. I'm fine." I tried to sit up and failed. "Just tell me."

"Kelly Hutchinson and Martin Cantrill were killed. Hutchinson on impact and Cantrill as he was trying to escape. He was shot. Kolbraski and John weren't injured but were captured. We don't know where they are now and the Texas Government isn't talking to us. The Ozarkian Intelligence Command has been waiting for you to wake up, to see if you had any info that could give them a lead on Mcgillicutty, Kolbraski and the others captured in that area."

"I'll help. I'll do whatever I need to do. I'll go into Texas if I have to. I know someone in Austin."

"Slow down Rob. In a few hours, I'll permit the intelligence team to come talk to you. After your parents have been here. But you can't overexert yourself yet."

"I feel fine."

"You don't just shake off a coma, Mr. Gehrig," chided Dr.

Katrinov, "but as soon as you're ready, the team wants you to begin working on finding Kolbraski and John and anyone else from that unit. So get your rest and save your strength so you can do a good job."

My parents came into the room and the military conversation ended.

KOLBRASKI - 5
Houston, Texas

After endless delays in what I figured out was Houston's Hobby Airport, the 55th Texas Shock Fighters were told the plane would be leaving San Antonio for El Paso. We hadn't been allowed to leave the plane the entire time on the ground. The Captain made up some story about the plane being equipped with amazing Texan technology that would make the flight to El Paso very short.

The flight took no time at all, further confirming in all our minds that we were always told lies. John began to hypothesize that the Flintstones would leave Bedrock to the East but I urged him to be quiet.

I overheard the word Houma as we landed but the windows were shaded and I wasn't quite sure where or what Houma was. We were all damn certain we weren't in El Paso.

The Captain got up and began shouting again.

"Ok Troops of the 55th Texas Shock Unit, you will disembark this plane and proceed no further than the water fountain at the end of the gate area, where you will await orders. You will be put in formation as you deplane. Row 1, UP."

The 'unit' deplaned and the Lieutenants marched us through the airport into a bus. All references to the airport's identity had been covered but I caught a picture of the New Orleans skyline on an ad. John saw the word 'Louisiana' peeking out of one covered flight schedule. None of this was conclusive, it being an airport, but it made it highly unlikely we were in El Paso.

The bus had covers over the windows but once we arrived at our destination it was obvious that the bayou we were in, was not the desert around El Paso.

The Captain had a pair of Sergeants issue swamp gear to the troops and then shouted at us again. I'd well-noted the fear tactics they used, merely covered up the fear they felt themselves. I sensed this fear and wanted to drive at it, to get it, knock it down and kill it.

"You are shock troops under guard of the Texas 55th regiment. From this point on, the penalty for disobeying orders is death by shooting. We are headed into a small town to secure it from terrorists. Your job is to proceed in front of the regiment and clear out any small resistance cells that may be encountered. If you attempt an unauthorized maneuver, you will be shot. If you are ordered to do something and fail to comply, you will be shot. If you seem to be performing below your ability, you will be shot. Is that clear. Let's march!"

Well, I guess that's clear. For the first few miles we met only small resistance cells. Usually a couple of farmers with rifles. Some fired, others didn't. We performed well below our ability, missing every farmer, but the Captain failed to punish. The worst scrap came when a group of about ten teenagers, armed with semiautomatics, began to spray fire from the ditch. Two prisoners and one regular, fell wounded. Medics carried the wounded regular to a medical truck but the shock troops were shot in the head and left behind. For the first time since being captured, the little monster inside me finally reared its ugly mug with indignity.

Who were these vile cretins to waste our lives so cheap? A pox upon them. I felt the lines of Henry V and Macbeth and King Lear and others racing through my head. I was moved to action but I held off for the right opportunity.

The Captain called a halt. "Baader!"

"Yes Captain!"

"Step forward."

Baader stepped forward and the Captain pulled out her sidearm.

"For failure to perform in battle to your ability." The Captain shot Baader through the head. Dead on between the eyes.

"You scabs better start aimin' better." The Captain laughed and the troops moved on. I about lost control. My two fallen comrades being shot while wounded and defenseless made it incredibly hard to keep control. The wanton assassination of Baader sent me over the edge. What if that had been John? Keeping my head about me had been my edge in training. Now I needed it, badly. I wanted to dip my sword in the blood of their sin and cut out the vileness within them. I'd take every last one of these Texans because I knew how to think and I smelled their fear. Plans within plans formed in my mind. Ghostly echoes of more reasonable thoughts were retired to more reasonable days. My reliance on Plato, Jung and Foucault gave way to Sun Tzu, Scipio and Patton.

After a few more miles, the unit came across a solitary man walking up the road in a gray cap, white shirt and jeans. He seemed to be unarmed.

The Captain ordered a halt.

"Friend or foe," shouted the Captain.

"Well that depends on who y'all are," replied the man.

"We're the 55th Texas Regiment, here on a mission to rescue the City of New Orleans from terrorists and Yankees."

A smile crossed my face as the Captain tipped her hand finally.

"Are you a friend of the south?" the Captain shouted.

A broad grin spread out across the man's face. "Ohhh yes. I AM a friend of the south. Very dearly. I've even heard tell there's some friends of the south left in Texas. You don't sound like you're one of them though, killing your own men, and Texas regimentin' all over the bayou."

Two other men appeared out of the ditches. A skinny white kid with a black T-shirt, camo pants and a gray cap shoved down over dreadlocks, and a huge broad shouldered black man in a muscle T, with dark shades, gray slacks and a camo cap worn backwards.

The Texan Lieutenants all watched the three men now. I eyed John. There was no time to plan. The opportunity was coming.

"We know how to deal with threats." The Captain stopped short, realizing no threat had been made.

"I'm sure you do," drawled the big man.

Suddenly about 300 soldiers emerged out of the swamp, carrying polished, well-oiled guns. Some dragged along rocket launchers. Speckled throughout, were men in regular US military uniform, some wore T-shirts and others had on fancy clothes. Nearly all wore gray caps. John and I exchanged startled glances.

The Captain gawked.

"See, we're the Volunteer regiments of the Garden District, French Quarter and City of Tuscaloosa, Alabama." The man in the white T-shirt directed his words at the mass of men behind him. "What's our regiment's number? Do we have a number boys?"

Out of the mumbling, a voice rang clear. "Oh, about three hundred and fifty," and the group broke out into laughter.

"My names, uh, Captain James Marlowe. You can call me Jeb though. What we're gonna do, is one of three things. The easiest is, you're going to leave your guns right where they are and turn around and walk right back down that road. The second is, we're gonna take your guns and you, back to New Orleans as prisoners. The third is," and Jeb's voice got louder and louder as he spoke, "you're gonna be idiotic and fight while outgunned 3 to 1 and we're goNNA KILL EVERY MOTHERFUCKIN LAST ONE OF YOU!!!" and the group let loose a frightening rebel war shriek.

As it quieted down, Jeb threw his final challenge at the Texas Captain. "Now, do you lay down your guns? Do you submit to the army of the New Confederacy? Or do we have a problem?"

As the Captain began to respond, I nudged John and began walking towards Jeb. I saw them swing their 350 weapons on me and laid down my gun. There'd be time to explain later. John followed, and soon, every one of the shock troops had laid down their guns and walked over to the side of the Confederacy. The Texas Captain yelled, "Halt!" over and over and was turning to give an order for the regulars to apprehend us, when one of the regulars let loose and fired.

Before either Captain could stop their squad, a barrage of fire began and the two armies retreated into battle formations. The shock troops, caught without guns, dispersed into the swamp. John and I took off, running low, stopping every ten feet or so at gunpoint to explain who we were and what we were doing. The Confederates had no idea the shock troops were prisoners. They got even angrier when they found out. They let us go, but wouldn't give us weapons.

We ran for an hour. Eventually, we were no longer stopped at gunpoint but had to leap to avoid corpses, littered here and there. Obviously, this wasn't the first action Marlowe's unit had seen. The battle dimmed in the distance. We walked into what looked like an old garage. We moved cautiously and found absolutely nothing but dirt. No old papers, no odd antiques, no trash. It didn't matter. We were exhausted and slept almost instantly upon hitting dry ground. The sun mercifully set and graced us with a moonless anonymous sleep.

The Sun - 5

The sun rose over the milling worried delegates at the UN in New York City. It crossed the planning, active leaders of the Midwestern and southern states, as they prepared for various contingencies. It crossed the desk of President Richard Morgan as he studied battle reports and sipped coffee. And it touched the cheek of Jeff Conroy who slumped in an airport chair, dreaming of a county fair that was so much better than anything he had experienced in his youth.

JEFF - 5
Pierre, Lakota Nation

A maintenance woman rolled a squeaky trash can through the airport gate and woke us up. As I stretched, Faye finally opened her eyes. I hoped our flight wouldn't be canceled again. The airlines routinely canceled flights into Denver and Colorado Springs now because of Texas air activity. The ground conflict was concentrated in southern Colorado but occasionally Texas air squadrons would strafe Interstate 25, north of Denver. After much debate, we had decided to try to fly into Sterling, Colorado, rent a car and drive down I-76. The Texans weren't bombing I-76, except near Denver. As we talked, the news came over the loudspeakers.

"For American Belief Radio in New York, I'm Greg Whitney. This is the Week In Review. Several more Native American groups in Arizona declared themselves independent today causing Texas to march into New Mexico. The Texas President announced his intention to save Arizona from anarchy. General Dale Bromberg of the Texas Army:"

"The main group, which calls itself Apache Nation, is not near as well organized or supported as the Lakota were. The Texan Army will end this in short order."

"The Texas Army had a busy week. They now occupy all of southern Kansas. The unoccupied northern counties have joined Nebraska. Texas also entered Colorado, Thursday, causing that state to join the Great Plains Alliance. On special assignment in Denver, George Halberstam has more."

"The Texan Army is decisively moving through Colorado in three main directions. They are, literally, driving up Interstate 25 towards Pueblo, where they may encounter some resistance. Another group is moving up the westernmost half of the state with the apparent intention of turning east at Grand Junction and heading towards Denver along I-70. And a third group is racing up the central west portion of the state through the Rio Grande National Forest, heading straight for Denver. There is no US military support or People's coalitions here. However, the Colorado Guard seems to be much better equipped than Kansas."

"When are the Texans expected to reach Denver, George?"

"I don't know Greg. It could be weeks, could be days."

"Thanks George. George Halberstam reporting from Denver, where the Colorado government awaits the invading Texas Army.

"Texas also tried to march into New Orleans Thursday but met with surprise resistance from troops of the New Confederacy. The states of Mississippi, Alabama and Georgia have formed a standing army to protect New Orleans and take back western Louisiana.

"Montana took over the administration of Idaho and Wyoming and temporarily seceded today. The Montanans are battling members of the terrorist group, Aryan Nation, in the hills of Idaho.

"Seven Midwestern states temporarily allied Monday and Tuesday and formed the United Midwestern States. They placed their headquarters in St. Louis and pledged to defend each other from the Chicago-Detroit alliance and Ozarkia. Michigan transferred its upper peninsula to Wisconsin for better administration until Chicago and Detroit are re-taken. Much of the Michigan government has been held hostage by troops of the Detroit rebellion.

"Small skirmishes were reported in Joliet and Aurora between Illinois National Guard troops and the Chicago Defense Group of the AAF. No major military movements were reported.

"Tuesday, Congressmen from New York, New Jersey and the New England states, left Washington temporarily. On Wednesday, those states withdrew their guard troops from federal control. Governor Kariachi of New York called these moves, 'temporary emergency measures.' The UN capital is in New York City.

"Steel Shevlin has a special report from New York City."

"The actions of New York and the New England states is the first taste New York City has had of the troubles out west. Citizens of the Big Apple had mixed reviews."

A man with a voice that belonged behind a deli counter said, "New York and New England are becoming one state, is that it?"

A woman with a sharp Bronx accent followed. "Yeah, I been to the Ozarks. What does that have to do with Senator Gray."

An obvious Brooklynite spoke next.

"Oh yeah! I been followin' dis whole thing on the net. Man I just hope New York doesn't get into it," he paused as someone informed him of something off mike, "Oh really? Damn! Well fuck 'em then."

A business-like woman with only a shade of New York accent said, "So can I still get to Jersey? There's another country for you! Ha."

Finally, a man with a Turkish accent said, "Yes I think it is very good. I am a good American."

Shevlin returned.

"Until the Texan Army takes the A Train or the Ozarkians invade

Times Square, New York won't be phased at all by the changes. I'm Steel Shevlin for American Belief Radio in New York."

"Troops of the Ozark People's Republic marched across the Mississippi into Memphis at noon on Wednesday. One hour later, Kentucky and Tennessee passed temporary bills of secession and formed the Ken-Ten alliance.

"Finally, a group of strongmen in Miami declared a dictatorship there. They emphasized Florida was to remain part of the US. Experts described the move as an attempt to control resources without risking reprisal. Troops of the New Confederacy have entered northern Florida with the intention of occupying the panhandle."

Along with the other 30 people in the airport, we raced to the ticket counters to see how this latest news would affect our tickets. We all knew the counter attendants would have nothing to tell us but we tried anyway. We didn't have anything else to do.

The attendant smiled and told us our tickets to Sterling were still good. She didn't have any idea whether the flight would be canceled, as she didn't know the plans of the Texas army. Faye laughed at that. We didn't have much longer to wait though and the attendant said that if we took off, we'd take off on time. That was slightly comforting.

We headed back to the gate to lean against each other and try to get some more rest before the next round of news.

STEVE - 9
New Mexico, I-10

We zoomed along I-10 for Arizona, quiet and apprehensive. I still didn't agree with Simone and Sam risking their necks, but Mulu had convinced everyone else it was necessary. Simone sat next to Mulu in the front seat. Helen sat in the back, in between Sam and me. We woke up early and had barely gotten out of Las Cruces before the Texans came.

"The Texan Army seems to like you Steve, they follow you wherever you go," needled Sam.

"How far to.... Where is it we're going?" I had forgotten already.

"Benson," said Mulu. "It's a little tourist trap outside of Tucson. The Californians are using it for an advance base. I'd say about two hours."

"So are the Californians on the Apache side?" Simone chimed in.

"Good question," answered Mulu, "I think they're more against the Texans, which certainly puts them on the... on some equitable level with the Apaches."

"What are we going to do when we get there?" I was wearying of Mulu's secrecy.

"Get you out," laughed Sam.

Mulu decided he could safely divulge his plan to us. "Hopefully, we can catch a flight to L.A."

"Can we stay with Mark in L.A.?" Helen turned to me.

"I don't know. I'll try to call him at the next gas station. Who knows where he is. He's a member of the California Peace Party."

"Checkpoint!" yelled Mulu.

Everyone tensed into silence. We had taken Simone's car particularly because she had real New Mexico plates. We had hoped to be waved through the checkpoint but the officer called for a stop.

"Good morning sir." Mulu used the gambit of speaking first.

The New Mexico Immigration Officer asked for Mulu's license. Mulu produced a fake New Mexico one, hoping it would pass.

"And yours ma'am," he indicated Simone. She handed him her real New Mexico driver's license.

"Traveling?" The Patrolman nodded towards Mulu.

"Yeah, headed to Benson to see the sights."

"Not a good day to be traveling in Arizona. Might want to stop in Lordsburg."

He eyed the three of us in the back seat. "How are you folks doing?"

We all agreed we were doing just fine, a little too loudly and quickly for the officer's taste.

"Where are you folks really going?" The Patrolman fixed a sympathetic gaze on me.

"We're fleeing the Texan Army," I blurted out as Mulu glared at me. "We need to get to Benson to hop a flight to L.A."

"Hopin' the Californians'll shelter you huh? What've ya done? Tried to vote? Think a thought, or worse tell someone about it? Ok, but I'm calling the APP Patrol to pick you up outside of Lordsburg on the Arizona side. They'll figure out what to do with you. Don't worry. I mean to safely keep you out of the action and get you on your way."

Mulu and Simone thanked the officer. Helen and I hugged in relief as Simone watched.

"That was close." Sam almost shouted to Simone.

"Yeah."

"Next stop, I need to call Mark," I said as Mulu sped on down the highway. We stopped at a gas station in Lordsburg. I went to phone Mark, and Sam went to check his mail at a public Deskset. Helen and Simone leaned against the car while Mulu pumped gas. I could barely overhear them, while Mark's phone kept ringing.

"You two be nice while I go pay," Mulu told the two women.

"What'd he mean by that?" Simone seemed honestly puzzled.

"Nothing," said Helen flatly.

"I'm sorry you don't... oh never mind." Simone turned to walk away.

"No. Don't worry about it. Just forget about it. I don't hate you. I think you're great."

Simone turned and gave an unconvincing thanks as Mulu walked up.

"Everybody happy? Good." He opened the doors for Helen and Simone.

I came back from the phone somewhat dejected. "No luck. Who knows where he is." I watched Helen getting in the front seat next to Mulu. So I plopped in next to Simone in the back. She left room for Sam on the other side.

Sam came back and got in the car with an update.

"Texans are in Cruces but all they did was station some troops in city hall and ask to be allowed to march through town. They're trying really hard to convince everyone they're just moving through New

Mexico to get to Arizona. They don't want any civil disruptions. Hell, everybody knows they could fly in all the troops they needed."

As we pulled out of the gas station, I heard a loud roar behind us. Both rear windows cracked apart and flew into the car. Simone dived on me and Sam dived on Simone.

After a few seconds, everyone sat up and looked at the billowing flame that had been the gas station. Mulu floored it and headed out of town.

"Thank god for protective glass."Helen looked at the harmless blue mosaic that had been her front seat window.

"Everyone ok?" shouted Mulu over the roaring engine.

"Sam? Sam!" Simone became horrified as she watched blood stream down Sam's side.

"I'm fine. Just got scratched by the window." Sam spoke weakly.

Mulu turned towards the back seat concerned. "Sam. No time to play around. If you're hurt we'll go the hospital no matter what's going on here."

"No, I'm fine." Sam's raspy voice sounded far from fine. "You know how I hate doctors. It's a lot worse than it looks. I mean it looks a lot worse than it is. Let's just get to Arizona quick."

I looked down at his side and caught a glint of metal, as he quietly pulled his coat around him.

Soon, we crossed the Arizona line.

"We're in no-man's land now," Mulu quietly observed.

All the other cars on the road had disappeared. No sounds stirred in the distance. The highway seemed dead, used up and discarded in front of us. Suddenly, a white car appeared from behind. It gained quickly and started flashing its headlights.

"I guess that's the APP. Pull over Mulu." Helen touched his shoulder.

"Yeah, I guess so huh?"

He pulled the car to the side of the road. The people in the white car had guns and asked everyone to get out and be searched. They moved us into the back of the white station wagon. One of them got in Sam's car to drive.

"This man needs medical attention." Mulu pointed at Sam.

"Just get in. We'll deal with that later." He shoved Mulu up into the station wagon.

As we moved onto the road, I could hear the driver conferring with a higher up. The gunmen said nothing about where we were going or why. None of our questions were answered. Mulu and Helen sat close on one side of the van. On the other side, Simone's hand slipped into mine. Sam bled quietly to himself.

KANDEL - 4
Benson, Arizona

"What!? Say that again!" The official California Peace Party command car was sorely in need of a tune-up. I could barely hear or be heard over the engine, as we bumped along a gravel road that wound up Lime Peak, outside Benson.

"Some Texan who says he knows you and is being sent to Benson. The APP picked him and some others up at the border on a tip from NM immigration. One of them seemed hurt."

"A Texan! I don't want any fuckin' Texans in Benson, except as prisoners."

"Is that an order?"

"You're damn right!" I was getting into the command stuff a little. Since I was more familiar with the situation than anyone and had good relations with Chief Wind, Reynolds had given me a spot promotion to Field Marshal and put me in charge of the Benson defense. I had no clue what I was doing but it felt good to yell at people and actually have them do what I said for once. "What was the other call?"

"The President of Mexico."

"What'd he want?" I was incredulous. Who did they think I was? Who was giving me this grand reputation as the Big Man in Arizona?

"Cessation of all hostilities near the Mexican border and a guaranteed safe zone."

Ah, push the new guy around, he's only an UNDERsecretary after all.

"So when does he want to meet about this and who does he want to talk to?"

"He wants a UN moderated meeting as soon as possible, between The Apache Chief, The Texan Ambassador and whoever is in charge of California Diplomacy."

"Who is that?" I sighed.

"You're the man from Diplomacy, sir."

"That's ridiculous! I'm the Undersecretary of Cultural Affairs. I warp the media. I have nothing to do, nor do I know, ANYTHING about warfare or diplomacy."

"Nonetheless, you're the boss," the aide admitted quietly.

When we got to the top of the peak, the soldiers began mapping battle plans, as I looked down towards New Mexico.

"Do you really think they'll cross into Arizona?"

Cameron, the aide, looked out over the desert floor. "Yes, if we let them. Maybe if they see us dug in though, they won't. But if we let one chink open, they'll be through it."

The soldiers relayed orders back to Benson and we immediately saw movement on the floor, as the California Desert 35th spread out along the I-10 corridor, to prevent the Texans from getting near Benson and Tucson. It suddenly hit me that Reynolds had put me in charge of the biggest and most important defense in the entire region. Were we that strapped for people? And I was also, apparently, the only operative even loosely linked to the Diplomacy Department, BUT, I wasn't complaining, just reeling.

When we arrived back in Benson, reports started flooding in as the Texas Army approached the border. Aides and Sergeants handled most of the work, while Commodore Vasquez's second in command, Captain Salimi, and I, nailed down the overall plan.

Salimi expressed a modicum of respect. "You're pretty good for an amateur. I don't think Vasquez could do much better himself."

"Tell it to the... actually don't tell anyone. As far as you know, I couldn't fight my way out of a paper bag. I don't want this job."

I was at my wits end, you know what I mean? I had a war and International relations thrown in my lap and I hadn't heard from Stephanie since she hung up on me. Cameron handed me some preliminary reports.

"Sir, the Texan prisoners are asking to see you. They claim they were running away from the Texan Army when they were arrested."

Oh GOD, I didn't want to deal with that. Who ARE these people? I stormed into the storage room where the prisoners were being held by two armed guards.

A familiar voice shouted at me from the back of the room. "Kandel, you idiot, I shoulda fired you, instead of letting you quit back at WPGU."

"Steve?" I shook my head to clear up the hallucination. "What are you doing here?"

"Getting out of Texas my friend... uh... could you..." He pointed to the guns.

"Yeah, they're free guys. Thanks.... Who are all these people?"

"Well this is my girlfriend Helen and this is my, uh, my friend Simone and this is our man in Denton, Mulu."

I shook Mulu's hand. "Good to meet you."

"This is Lieutenant Mark Kandel of the--"

"Field Marshal," I said grinning like a dead monkey. "I'm a Field Marshal just like Goering." I shook my temporary rank insignia.

Steve stepped back. "My, aren't we oppressing up in the world."

"Yeah, well when you have ideals you can go places in this man's army," I cackled.

"So... I mean what's the deal with that?" Steve indicated the insignia.

"UH, the guy in charge out here got shot and since I was around they asked me to stop planting propaganda and start directing warfare."

"Listen Mark, there's one more guy with us. Simone's boyfriend Sam. He was pretty badly hurt in Lordsburg but they wouldn't let us do anything about it until we got here. They took him off somewhere for medical attention but... you know, we need to know if he's all right."

I turned to a guard and asked him to check on it.

"So, are we going to be able to get out of here?" Steve looked anxious.

"That depends." I wanted to let him down slowly.

"On what?"

"On the Texans... and the UN... oh, and probably the Mexicans. For the next 24 hours though, I'd say no... unless you wanna risk getting shot in a war zone."

They all sat back down in their chairs.

The guard came back and reported on their friend Sam's situation. I confered with him outside the room then went back in to relay the news.

"They say they pulled enough metal out of his side to make a Buick but he's resting comfortably. He must have lost a lot of blood. I'll check in on him and let them know it's all right for you to visit him.

The tall girl, I think her name was Simone, sank down into a chair her head in her hands. The hurt guy was her man I think. Steve went quickly to her and put his arm around her to give some comfort. I may be mistaken as I didn't know the rest of them very well, but Steve's girlfriend seemed awfully bothered by this.

"Listen, I'm sorry, but anything you want that we can get you is yours. Just talk to the guard outside the planning office, his name is Kyoto. I've got to go call the President of Mexico, then I'll check on Sam."

STEVE - 10
Benson, Arizona

"Thanks Mark," I said as Kandel left.

"Let's go get some food." Helen grabbed me by the arm, literally dragging me out of the room.

"Hey! Not so hard. I'm coming. Where are we going anyway?"

"I don't know. To that guard guy. That's not really why I grabbed you."

"Ok, why?"

"What is going on between you and Simone?" She looked at me blankly.

"Nothing. I told you a long time ago that nothing is, has or ever will be going on between me and Simone."

"Then why all the glances and smokes on the porch and and touching and stuff?"

"We're close friends Helen. She likes to talk to me about stuff that she doesn't want to talk about in front of everyone. And right now she needs someone to talk to, bad."

"I'm sorry Steve. I guess you're right about right now, but I just wasn't buying it before. I'm beginning to think... I don't know. You're being honest with me?"

"Yes." I was exasperated. We really didn't need this right now. "You want the UN to handle this when they get here?"

"Stop. You're hurting my feelings Steve."

"I'm sorry." I lowered my voice. "It's just that I don't see how I'm ever going to get you to forget about me and Simone."

"I'm trying but you're not making it easy."

"Well, I'll work on it but I'm still going to be Simone's friend. Especially now. Geezus Helen, I wouldn't hit on her in front of you with her boyfriend, my friend, a bloody mess in a makeshift hospital room. Now let's go get that food like we said."

KOLBRASKI - 6
New Orleans, Louisiana

Pat and I woke up on the floor of the garage, dirty, sore and hungry. We wandered outside and down a road for awhile. Eventually we lucked out and caught a ride with an elderly gentleman from New Orleans. He agreed to drive us into town, no questions asked.

"Ah know yeh ain't got no money boys. But I can tell an honest case when I see one. I'm Pete Riley."

Soon, we were getting off the highway and Riley was about to let us off at Canal St.

"Now you boys be careful. I heard 'bout some a that fightin' over near Houma. Trouble. Trouble. Trouble. Tell yew what. Here's the address of a place where you can stay. They'll set yuh up nice and purty. Getcha on yo way. Yew jus' tell 'em Smilin' Pete Riley gave yeh the nod. They'll take care of yuh."

We thanked him and stumbled, bewildered and dirty, towards the French Quarter.

"I don't know if we should go to this place or not. Could be a setup," John warned.

"No. He went too far out of his way for that. It's real. But I don't see why we can't go grab a beer before we go there."

"No wonder they put you in charge. I knew you were good for something."

"You're buyin' right?"

"Hell!" John realized we didn't have any money. "I guess we should go straight to the mystery date then huh?"

I bent down to tie my shoe and stood up holding five 50s half hidden in my palm. John gaped.

"Always think ahead John. When will I ever teach you anything?"

"Shut up Kolbraski. Where are we going to go? Even five 50s won't get us into one of the nice bars and the French Quarter's cheap bars have gotten really bad."

"Nothing could be worse than what we've been through. Let's head to the water and pick a dive."

We walked through the glistening, restored part of the Quarter and out into a section near the water which hadn't received much attention since the fire of '05. About a block and a half along the waterfront, we found an open establishment.

The bar occupied a two-story brick building that looked untouched by the fire. A wooden sign with a bare bulb shining on it read, 'The Slowdown Bar & Grill--Since 1997.' A sign in the window advertised the long extinct Miller Genuine Draft.

John opened the wrought iron door and we entered the smoky, dark interior. A 'Slick' band was breaking down their equipment on a stage immediately to the left. Empty tables sat on a dusty floor in front of the stage. To the right, four people sat at the bar drinking pints.

I went to the bar and the bartender sauntered over. She stood taller than me, but I couldn't tell if it was because I was short or she was on an elevated platform. She had jet-black hair, streaked with purple, cut short below the ears and wore an old work shirt and jeans. She had deep brown eyes that spoke volumes without telling you a thing.

She looked at me with a hostile but polite expression and said, "Do you want something?"

"Yeah. I'd like two pints of Bud." I looked her straight in the eye.

The bartender gazed smoothly and benignly from me to John and back.

"Can I see your I.D.'s?"

"No." I said it as firm as a preacher.

"Well, then no beer." She gave a quick smirk and turned away.

"Wait ma'am?"

She stopped and turned slowly. "What."

I held a 50 out towards her.

Her lips formed a cold smile. "You trying to bribe me?" She moved back towards us. "You're gonna need more than that."

"Well, yeah."

We stared each other down for a few seconds.

"Not that I couldn't use the money but honestly you look like trouble and I don't need trouble so why don't you just blow." She held her gaze on me.

"I don't want to go off on a sob story but my friend and I had our I.D.'s taken and we slept last night in a garage in the swamp. We don't know a soul in town, except a vague reference from some guy named Riley, and so--"

The bartender cut me off. "Smilin' Pete Riley?"

"The very one." I lifted my head up hopefully.

"Ok. And?"

"And godda... and we just want to sit and have a beer and forget about all the shit we've been through and all the shit we're going to go through and just... relax."

"Do you own this place?" John stopped looking around and began paying attention.

"Yeah." The bartender shifted her gaze to John.

"If we tip well and behave ourselves and engage in witty repartee with the owner, will it score us any points and get us on our way to a beer?"

The bartender cracked a smile. "Maybe."

"Well my friend Mack here has the tip, you've got the beer and I promise to behave both of ourselves. Whaddaya say?" John smiled big.

"What about the witty repartee?" She cocked her head and looked amused.

John played along. "I'll owe you. I'm much wittier after a beer."

"Aren't we all." The bartender put on a pseudo-mysterious look. She turned away this time to draw the beers. I laid the 50 on the table and looked around. The two men closest to us had turned back to their conversation, oblivious to the rest of the bar. At the far opposite end, a man sat staring into his beer and a woman sat just beyond him, leaning back, staring holes in John.

The bartender came back with the beers and looked at the 50. "Put that away. It's dangerous. I'll run a tab. Hell, I'll probably pay it. I'm Darlene. Who are you and what's your story. How do you know Smilin' Pete Riley?"

"I'm Mack and this is John. We don't really know Smilin' Pete all that well. We just met him today. We're escaped prisoners of the Texas Army, who got caught in the melee outside Houma."

At the mention of the Texas Army, the woman at the opposite end of the bar stiffened and turned the heat of her glare up a notch. The man sitting next to her put a hand on her shoulder and nodded.

"You got caught by Marlowe's regiment then, right?" Darlene wiped down the bar as she spoke.

"Yeah, but the fight was chaos so we ended up running and sleeping in an abandoned garage. Smilin' Pete Riley picked us up and gave us a ride into the city. He gave us an address to go for help."

"That sounds like Pete. He's a good guy and a good judge of character. Mentioning his name did more good for you here than that bullshit about witty repartee." She looked humorously at John.

"Just let me finish my beer."

"Yeah?" Darlene half smiled and returned to the other end of the bar to wash some glasses.

We quietly drank our beers. The woman at the other end still glared at us from time to time. She had blonde hair and ruby red lips and when she looked mean, she meant it. Once in a while, she looked at the man next to her and whispered something in his ear. He just kept looking in his beer and nodding with his lips pursed.

Darlene finished the glasses and went over to the disc player and put on some Slick music.

"What is this?" John winced.

"It's a local band called the Couldabeens," answered Darlene. "A bunch of drunks who play just well enough to play Slick. Occasionally they get good enough to pull off some old Punk songs too. They do incredible covers of old 90's songs. Uncle Tupelo, Replacements, shit like that."

"Replacements are more 80's," John corrected.

"Yeah." Darlene thought. "Kinda both I guess. It's just that whole era they like to cover."

John stood. "You wanna dance?"

"You can dance?" Darlene smirked.

"No. He can't. He's got clubs for feet." I felt marginally jealous.

"Yes." John really wanted to dance.

"All right let's see." Darlene held out a hand.

"Come out from behind the bar." John commanded.

"This better be better than your repartee."

She came out from the bar and walked out on the floor, looking at John expectantly. John began to gyrate like a belly dancer, and boy did he have the belly. I cackled. The two men sitting in the middle of the bar began to clap along Slick style. The glaring woman looked disgusted.

Darlene began to dance along much more smoothly and elegantly. I about fell off my barstool. Glaring woman couldn't take it anymore. She got up and yelled at John.

"You disgust me! I hate you pieces of shit. Why don't you get the fuck out of here. Go crawl back into some hole!"

The man with her still sat staring at his beer, lost in the bubbles.

Darlene stopped dancing and took the woman back to her barstool.

"Come on Joann. Leave the guy alone. Ok? No trouble."

"There wasn't going to be any trouble till you let these two shit faces in the bar. What are you thinin' Darlene?"

Darlene sat Joann down at the bar and turned around. John followed them.

"Look, just ignore her. Ok? Don't.... Just let it go. Ok?"

John slid around Darlene.

"Hey!" Darlene lunged at him and missed.

"I just want to buy her a beer." John looked over his shoulder. "Let me buy you a beer Ma'am. Can I buy you a drink? I don't know what you've got against me but I don't think I deserve it. Let's just be cool. Let me buy you a beer."

The woman smoldered and yelled at the man she was with.

"Hey Jerry, should I let this drunk buy me a beer?"

"Yeah. Why not? He can buy me one too." The muttering man didn't look up from his beer.

John smiled. "Good. Two beers for the happy couple here. On me."

"On me," I corrected, a bit miffed at John's generosity.

"Fuck you all." Darlene went to draw two more beers.

After a while, Darlene, John and one of the men at the middle of the bar, named Tom, got into an intense discussion about sports. John loved sports but I could care less. I hated it when he sat in front of the television when we could be out in the sunshine.

John held that St. Louis had the best chance to improve in the draft while Tom argued New Orleans only needed a good Running Back. Darlene told them they were all fucked and continually tried to prove football was much less worthwhile than drinking. I kept quiet. I'd learned to let John and his sports alone.

At 2:00, Darlene closed the bar and ushered everyone out. We said our good-byes to Tom and his friend Al.

Darlene saw us out the door. "You boys be careful. Just go straight to that address Riley gave you. You'll be fine."

She hugged John and shook hands with me.

"And if you get a chance before you blow, stop back in the Slowdown."

John assured her we would and made a lame attempt to ask her to come along with us which, thank God, she brushed off deftly.

"I think she likes me," said John as we walked down the street toward the center of the Quarter.

"I think she likes your drinking capacity and my 50 dollar bills," I shot back spitefully. Why was John so loose?

Two more steps and I felt something bite into my ear. Suddenly I heard water rushing all around me. I wondered if we had gotten too close to the docks and fell in the water. But we'd been going toward the center of town. It didn't make any sense. I tried to swim but I couldn't see anything and moving didn't make any difference. The rushing got louder and louder. I could still breathe but the streetlights seemed to have gone out.

A man called my name in the distance. I could barely make out a robed figure. He bowed his head toward me and amidst the roar, repeated over and over again, "resist."

The man disappeared and the roar began to calm and break up into voices. I couldn't distinguish one from another but it sounded like a room full of late night talk show hosts delivering mediocre monologues to an overeager audience.

Slowly I began to see light and a softball of nausea hit me square in the gut. The roar thinned to nothing, leaving voices and the sounds of office work. I tried to open my eyes but they were clamped down. After a struggle, I began to see more lights and felt my eyelids separate like Tupperware.

After a minute, shapes formed out of the light and I could make out a man in uniform, sitting close to me. John was asleep, or passed out, in the next chair.

The uniform noticed me and spoke. "Well, sailor, how's your head?"

I felt my temple and came across the traces of a heat suture. My shirt glowed red with blood. John was in marginally better shape, with two Band-Aids on his chin.

"All right, let's go. Where to boys?"

Another officer came up and shook John onto his feet.

Still drunk and dazed, I tried to tell them where but couldn't make the words travel through my cortex to the speech centers. The echoes of the robed man still dominated my mind. I felt the monster in me coming to life but for the first time, not with rage. It spoke an unbroken soliloquy in the back of my mind, like a sermon or a chant. I kept hearing the word, resist.

"Any ID?" The officer held John.

"No." The uniform looked at us with indifferent disgust. "Tankers I'd guess. Let's take 'em to the Bahrain."

"But that's US. Will they take them?"

"They're hard up these days. They'll take anybody."

The officer got up and jerked me to my feet, jump-starting my optic nerve and somewhat clearing my head. The one holding me wore a Louisiana State Police uniform and had a bushy black mustache with shocking blonde hair. The officer holding the half-conscious John was thinner and had wiry brown hair. He also had a badge and a nametag that read 'Sgt. Ranier.'

A voice rang in from out of my sight range. "Lieutenant Copston. Your car is ready."

"All right." Lieutenant Copston got in my face and shouted. Where did you say your hotel was?"

I tried to think how to tell them about the address which John had on him. Nothing came out right. "Mrr frggg hss aggrttss."

"That's what I thought. Let's go."

They dragged us out to a squad car and began to drive. Now and then I heard the words 'pier' and 'tanker' and slowly realized we were heading toward a big Navy boat. I tried to jerk John into consciousness. He burbled and gurgled but made no sense. Finally, I rifled through his pockets and found the address.

"Look..." I leaned toward the glass that separated us. "I've god thuh Aggress."

"What's he saying?"

"Something about a dress."

Copston smiled. "Settle down sailor. We'll have you on your boat in no time."

"Ime nog a sailor. Loog. I hava plakes to skay." I thrust the card up in the window.

Copston chuckled. "He certainly isn't making much sense is he?"

"I think he really does have a place to go though. This address is on St. Andrew's. Isn't that Pete Riley's Stead?"

"No shit. The sailor knows Riley, huh? Ok. We'll take him to Riley then. That's a helluva lot easier than fucking around with the goddamned US Navy."

The policemen dumped us out in front of an old brick building with a sign that said 'Riley's Federal Homestead. Acceptable Guests Only. No Trespassing.'

They waited to see if we got kicked out on our cans. I dragged John to the admittance window and showed the woman the card.

"Where'd you meet up with Smilin' Pete?"

"On the road between here and Houma this morning."

"Oh you're the ones. Where the hell have you been?"

She buzzed the door open and the cops drove away.

"You're a mess. I'll show you to 186. Just clean up a bit and get some rest. We'll talk to you tomorrow." John regained a handle on mobility but still couldn't talk. The woman showed us into a room, turned on the lights by the bed and in the bathroom, gave me a key and left.

The next morning we took showers and crawled downstairs to the main room for breakfast. A handful of people sat at tables in a room the size of a battleship. I recognized the woman who had showed us to our rooms the night before.

"Ah, you look in much better shape this morning." She shook our hands. "Smilin' Pete wants to see you. After breakfast, just go in through those south double doors and announce yourself to the secretary."

I thanked her and we sat down and gorged ourselves on beignets, eggs, bacon and coffee. No one at the table seemed interested in conversation. Afterwards, we headed to the double doors. A woman in a pink taffeta dress sat at a flat desk facing the doors.

She looked up as we walked in. "Oh.... Uh, Don." She got up quickly and walked through a side door. "Don, there's some people here."

"Ok, Chin. I'll be there in a minute. Try greeting them and being nice for once," said a gravelly voice on the other side of the door.

"Oh shut up." She sounded as much amused as annoyed.

She came back and put on a smile for us.

"Don will be with you in a minute. He's the secretary to Mr. Riley. I don't actually work here. I'm Pete's wife. Chin-ye Mao." Her bright smile warmed my heart.

"As in Mao Zedong?" I shook her hand.

"Who knows?" she said genially. "I might as well be related to Churchill."

"Well it'd be something either way."

John stepped up. "I'm John, John Mcgillicutty. And my rude friend here is Mack Kolbraski."

"No. No. Not rude at all." Chin smiled.

Don came walking out from the side door. He stood about six-foot with a shaved head and bright blue eyes. He wore a silk shirt and black coat, wing tips and a fedora. The vision of the robed man flooded my mind again. Resist. Resist. Resist.

"Pardon my rudeness ma'am, but I had some difficulty yesterevening." I hardly recognized my own voice.

"I see we're all making friends." Don smiled like a cat. "I'm Don DeJee. Pete has a friend of his in the office right now, who wants to meet you. Come on in."

Don led the way and turned before opening the door marked 'Smiling Pete Riley--Consultant.' "Can you watch the front Chin?

Thanks." He went through the door before she had a chance to say anything.

Smilin' Pete sat at a large ebony desk drinking a mint julep. In a chair to the right of the desk sat the man in the gray cap, who had led the Confederate army against Texas. Smilin' Pete stood and greeted us warmly. Don exited quietly.

"Ah. Mr. Kolbraski. Mr. Mcgillicutty. Pleasure to see y'all agin. Ah b'leeve yew know Captain Marlowe here. Though I don't b'leeve you've been formly introduced."

Marlowe looked even darker up close than he had in the field. He had closely cropped black hair under his gray cap, straight bushy black eyebrows and the cold steel glare of a killer in the cause of good. He reminded me of the portraits of the Saracens who defended Palestine against the Crusaders.

"I do recognize you two." He spoke in a lower, deeper voice than he'd used on the battlefield. "You were the first two to drop your guns and move. I'm glad you made it out."

Smilin' Pete moved around the desk to a bar.

"Can ah fix you boys a drink? D'yew like a Julep now and again?"

We both agreed to a Julep and sat down. Smilin' Pete looked at the glass.

"'And first behold this cordial Julep here. That flames, and dances in his crystal bounds.' Ah man by the name a Milton said that. Fine poet. Fine drink. Now." Riley settled into his chair. "Captain Marlowe and I feel quite awful about the Texans pressing prisoners into service. We would like nothin' better than to get you boys back home. But, relations bein' what they are with the north, 'specially Kentucky and Tennessee, unfortunately, I can't see no way now."

"That leaves you two options." Marlowe leaned forward. "You can either wait it out here in Mr. Riley's general employ, until arrangements can be made to get you home. Just so you know, that will expose you to more fighting near New Orleans. Or you can spend a few days making some quick money in Mr. Riley's Gaming establishments and hit the road east, to try and hitch up through the Carolinas and hit a plane home from Asheville."

I sipped my Julep and looked up at Marlowe. Resist. "What kind of fighting do you mean if we stay?" I resisted the urge to call him 'good sir', for some reason.

"Well, the New Confederacy has them held well outside of Houma now. They counted on a lot of surprise with those shock troops you were in and left them ill supported. But they're regrouping for another push as soon as the New Mexico trouble settles down. Mr. Riley provides civilian support for the troops. If they get into or near New Orleans you might be picked up by them and hauled off back to Texas or who knows what," Marlowe finished with a grim look.

"What are these Gaming establishments?" John leaned forward.

Pete smiled. "Your basic Internet, Virchule Rality, Role-Playin type things. We specialize in some hard-to-get scenarios, see. Some that b'fore this here war, were a little, you might say, unapproved."

I finished my Julep and set it down on the coffee table in front of me. It seemed to go right to my head. I felt wavy. "We'll have to talk this over. When do you want or need to know?"

"Weel, If you wanna stay, you can stay. No hurry on that. Captain Marlowe here is headed back to Alabama now. If you had a mind to go now, you can get as far as Tuscaloosa with him. However 'f yew wanna stay and work the Game rooms some b'fore you go. Well, I don't see any harm in that either. You can head when you like."

Marlowe stood up. "I'm leaving tonight. If you want a ride, just meet me at the Hyatt, before nine. Otherwise, I'll catch yuh later. Oh, and I have something for you. We found these on the battlefield with a bunch of other things the Texans abandoned. It might do you more harm than good but I thought you might want them." He handed us our Ozarkian I.D.'s.

We shook hands with Marlowe. "We'll let you know our plans by five." John nodded agreement.

This pleased Smilin' Pete. "Excellent. Jes ring up *88 on any phone in the place and if I'm not here, leave a message."

Marlowe exited without saying another word. We followed. Smilin' Pete closed the door behind us, wishing us well. Chin still sat at the desk and said goodbye as we left.

We sat back down in the dining room and had some more coffee.

"I don't know, John. Maybe it's that Julep but I feel funny about this whole thing. I think we should strike north and get back to Arkansas. We've gotta resi... resist the Texans. We aren't doing anybody any good, headed east."

"C'mon Kolby. That's suicide. If we strike out east, we can at least get back safely and then rejoin. We're no good dead."

"Yeah, I guess you're right John. I just... feel dead already. Or like a part of me is dead. Like the redemption of Augustine."

"What?"

"I don't know, John. I've gotta get some fresh air. I'll be right back."
John reached out and touched me on the arm. "Kolby? You ok?"
"Yeah, I'm fine."
"Don't be gone long, ok?"
"Don't worry John." I leaned down and kissed him and felt like I was saying goodbye.

Outside didn't make me feel any better. The air was thick with mucous. People whirled around me, headed to and fro in a city of sin. That's what was bothering me. This city of sin and disgrace, keeping me from my holy vow to fight the Texans. Resist. Of course.

I walked several blocks and saw a man in dark robes, leaning against a voodoo shop. I had to know who he was. "Are you with the shop?"
"No."
"Are you the one I was to meet?" I hardly knew what I was saying. I felt the monster's soliloquy merge with my voice.
"Perhaps. Who are you?"
"I'm Mack Kolbraski, defender of the Arkansans."
"Hmm. So, what is it you want? Did someone send you?"
"Yes, he said, 'resist'. I need to get to Arkansas."
"Right. Shhh. We shouldn't talk here. Come with me."
The robed figure led me down the street and into a basement. Candles were lit on every side, giving the place an angelic red glow.

Another robed figure sat in the corner. The one who led me there said, "This man knew the password. He wants to get to Arkansas."
"I wasn't aware we had anything there. But utmost secrecy is important in our little venture. Very good. Conduct him to the station."

The first robed man motioned for me to follow him. We went through several candlelit rooms, until we came to a library. He moved some shelves out of the way and gave me a package.
"Resist my friend. Good luck in your journey. This tunnel leads you to the station. Tell the driver your destination and he will take you."

I wandered down the tunnel for what seemed a mile before I saw a light. I had no idea what the package was. It had been entrusted to me, I thought, I should only have faith. My head was pounding now. I had a hard time keeping my balance.

The tunnel emptied out in an underground parking garage, full of men waiting by unmarked trucks. One of them approached me.
"Resist. You have a package. Where to?"
"Arkansas."
"That's a new one. All right climb in. It'll be a trick getting you into

Tennessee but we'll do it."

I felt woozy and fell asleep. The Julep had hit me much harder than it should.

I woke, extremely parched and staring into the sun.

"Hey! You finally awake! We're almost to Memphis. If you hadn't breathed so heavy I woulda thought you was dead. There's water on the floorboard."

I reached down and guzzled water. My head still hurt but I felt a little better.

"I'm gonna drop you off just outside of Southaven, on the line. It's the only chink in the Memphis border control. They've got Arkansas locked up tight. You'll have to fake your way through Memphis and across the bridge. I hear taking a cab, strangely enough, is the easiest way to do it. You ok?"

I looked at the pilot and saw a brave comrade-in-arms. He deserved honor. "My cause is holy and just my friend, and you will be rewarded."

"Yeah, I don't know about that, but I been paid pretty good, don't worry. You sure you're ok?"

"My steps do lead aright. I'm fine. Just road weary. Much traveling ahead. Goodbye."

I leaped out of the truck and began walking down the road into Memphis, Tennessee. The sun watched me closely and protected me. These trials were well worth the fight I'd be able to give the Texans. Resist. I reflected on the strange turn of events that landed me here. Only divine guidance could explain the dream that led me to the cloaked man.

Poor John. Poor, poor John. It was God's will to lead me away from him but I missed him dearly. Still, I felt different now. Released. Strangely new in my mind. The whole of my experience up till now had been a purgatory of fire, a crucible to harden me for the battle. The Ozarkians didn't know what aid they were about to fall into.

Suddenly, I was surrounded by Ken-Ten guards.

"Put up your hands!"

They vilely placed their hands on me and took the package with which I'd been entrusted. "Damn."

"Yeah, It's coke. C'mon you."

I saw through their veiled ruse and also saw their stealth copter nearby. It sat silent and full of motion like a divine gift. Damn. They'd spilled the contents of the package. No matter. The package of my person was much more valuable. The four of them began to force me along. I saw with divine clarity. I was forged anew and they knew not.

I slumped. In that moment, as if with six eyes I saw each one of them yield into an indefensible position and with more limbs than I possess, scattered them and ran for the copter. They shot at me but I was invulnerable.

"Hail Ozarkia, The People and St. Alban!" I cried as I raised the copter toward heaven.

JEFF - 6
20,000 Feet over Lakota Nation

"And thank you for flying Lakotair operated by Southwest." The flight attendant finished the safety demonstration and packed away her props. The plane left Pierre behind and we settled back into our seats and began the ritual of wasting air time. The flight to Sterling, Colorado normally took a little over an hour. Lakota Nation employed the latest T-Jet designs in all its planes. A combination of partnerships and slick dealing, quickly gave the young nation a nice fleet of passenger planes.

As I looked out the window, I noticed something very wrong. I turned to Faye. "Look down there."

"Yeah, it's far." Faye smirked.

"Far down and far from where we want to be, that's Mt. Rushmore."

"So?"

"So, we should be going south, not west."

"Maybe there's some flight pattern stuff where you can't go south until, well you know what I mean. Everything's messed up right now."

"Yes, and I'm fairly sure that's not it. I think we're being hijacked. We're well west of Sterling now and actually heading a bit north."

"Should we tell an attendant?"

"You'd think they'd already notice."

I flagged an attendant and began to ask her about our location.

"Sir, could you come with me?"

"Why?" I was suspicious.

"Your question is interesting and my long explanation, I'm sure, would DISTURB the other passengers."

"Oh." I suddenly understood. I got up and went toward the back of the plane to the galley. Faye followed.

"We're not on a heading for Sterling. The Captain is a Montana native and has decided he could much better serve humanity and his country by flying this plane to Missoula and volunteering for the Great Plains Army."

"Where does that leave us? Has he thought about that? Huh?"

"You will be in Missoula, Montana, like the rest of us. The Lakota Nation will most likely negotiate a quick settlement with Montana over return of the plane."

"What about getting to Colorado?"

The attendant looked fiercely indifferent. "I have no idea. Now I have to serve drinks."

Faye gaped at the attendant's calm. We returned to our seats in fuming silence, listening to the rumble of the plane as I ticked off the landmarks below.

STEVE - 11
Benson, Arizona

We'd seen Sam, and he didn't look good. Of course, he told us not to worry and that we should see what the other guy looked like. The doctor said he was critical, still, and had lost a lot of blood. He also told us we did the right thing in bringing him straight to Benson, because the hospital in Lordsburg had burned down yesterday. The doctor only allowed us to see Sam for a minute and told us to come back later

I sat with my head against the Deskset speaker. An announcer droned out some dry commentary about the Arizona Council for Virtual Mobility. Mark had stopped in earlier with an update on the political situation. Most all of the California defenses had held against the Texans and little actual combat had occurred. All skirmishes ended this morning at ten when a UN mandated general cease-fire took effect. So far, the Mexican troops had stayed behind their border.

Now Mark was off at a meeting to try and end this thing. He promised to phone as soon as he determined the possibility of leaving Benson. Meanwhile, Mulu played a computer strategy game and Helen and Simone played a somber game of rummy. The commentary ended and the news broke in.

"For American Unity Radio, I'm Greg Whitney. Emergency negotiations are underway between the governments of California, Texas and Mexico to prevent Mexican troops from entering the conflicts in the southwest. Rebelling Native Americans in Arizona have toppled the Arizona state government. Texas has invaded New Mexico and parts of Arizona. California is aiding the Native Americans. As of this date, the Mexican border has not been breached but Mexico is demanding a neutral zone be set up to prevent the fighting from endangering Mexican citizens.

"This is American Unity Radio.... Pray for peace."

HANK - 3
Nogales

I stood at a phone booth and watched the California diplomat Mark Kandel walk into the conference room. He took a seat next to UN Negotiator Alaine Pascual and across from Mexico's Secretary of State, Maria Altera Alou.
I tried to end my conversation with President Morgan.

"Look, Mr. President, we're going to have to give something here to get something. That's all I'm saying."

From over the plains and hills, Morgan's voice resonated. "Dammit, Hank, I didn't give you this position to give ground but to get it. We don't have to take nothing outside of New Mexico but New Mexico is Texas now. You understand? And we aren't budging on that."

"And if I have to avoid war?"

"Then I, with trembling and regret, think of the lives those governments will waste on the battlefields of theft. For our land is sacred and will not be taken from us. Listen Hank, I know you're going to give a little and I'll live with it. But an inch not a yard. Give 'em rocks and desert, not streams and life. Understand?"

"Yes, Mr. President. I understand."

"Good Luck Hank. Do right." President Morgan rang off.

I whispered into the dead phone, "Which is it. Do right or follow orders?"

I turned and walked into the conference room. For most of the meeting, I sat idly by as Pascual proposed several divisions of the land in question. I kept looking for the United States representative to object on the grounds that all this land was theirs. Finally, I realized there was no US representative. Either through ignorance, bureaucratic bungling, or pride, they had failed to send someone, so Pascual was proceeding as if they didn't matter.

It didn't matter to me. The talk with Morgan had put me in a mood of general apathy. I hated the expansionist policies but even more, I hated the way Morgan dressed them up in fine words and false patriotism. The true Texans didn't want all this. Was I a true Texan?

Finally, the time came for me to pipe up with Morgan's party line.

"My government asserts its historic right to all of New Mexico and to remain peaceful, requires that no breach of that State's borders occur."

Kandel looked annoyed and Alou stared at me hard. I looked down.

Alou broke the silence first. "I'm sorry Ambassador Connely, but Mexico has a much better historic claim on that region. The name if nothing else gives that away. Let me tell you what we propose."

She got out a pointer and began delineating a wide area to be used as a safe zone for Mexico.

When she was finished, Kandel exclaimed, "My God Alou. You want half the Southwest. Why don't we just give you Colorado too. Refunding the Gadsden Purchase would make more sense."

Alou didn't waver and looked Kandel directly in the eyes. "All right. Let's make that the basis of our negotiations. Mr. Connely?"

"Doesn't sound like a bad idea at that." I thought about the historical imperative behind the forced purchase of Gadsden and how I could make it play well with Morgan. Hell, Morgan could buy it back from them fair and square after this was all over and right a great wrong. Was I becoming as bad as him?

"Fine. Somebody get a history book. We'll need a good map." Kandel sighed.

The conference proceeded well after this point, using the Gadsden borders as a jumping off point and tweaking it here and there to make a balanced modern agreement. Instead of running along the Gila River as it did before the Gadsden purchase, the border would run south of Interstate 10, leaving Tucson in California. This suited Mexico's desire for a safety zone without having to gain any large cities to administer. It didn't take any large swaths from California or Texas. Mostly 'desert and rocks' as Morgan had requested.

The group recessed before the signing, to consult with their heads of state. I reached Morgan at home in his luxury bath, eating caviar and Ritz crackers. I pitched the Gadsden idea to him. He didn't like it.

"Gadsden? But we bought Gadsden fair and square from the Mexicans back in the 1800's. We needed it to run a railroad, if I remember correctly."

I knew I'd run up against this. The President had an acute historical sensibility. I sort of wish he'd have it removed. But I was also counting on Morgan reclining in that bath with a tumbler of Martini's fuzzying his historical prowess. That would help bring us to equal levels.

"Well, we didn't buy it, Mr. President, the US did. And secondly, they basically forced a financially desperate Santa Anna, to sell at gunpoint. We'd deliver it back to them from the clutches of the Yankees."

I risked a quick breath before delivering my next point. I didn't want him to think about the name Santa Anna for long. "And besides, if we wanted to buy it back from them later, we'd right a great wrong and restore balance to the region." I tried not to breathe heavy, as I waited for Morgan's response. I heard the tinkle of ice and the slosh of water.

"Yeah I suppose we could." His voice trailed off again.

"Could what?" I was thrown off.

"Could take it back from them later. Just keep 'em quiet for now. Sort of loan it to them out of our good hearts."

"Well, I don't think they'll accept it that way sir." Jesus this man was twisted.

"Oh hell, Hank I know that. I wasn't born into diplomacy yesterday. I know what you're up to and I think it's fine. I'll tell the General Staff to leave off Gadsden from the Western movement and start drawing up a plan to take it back at a later time. This time for Texas. Hell, we could even pay for it again just like the US. Just to make it all fair and square. Good work Hank. I knew you'd pull through for me. We're going to make a great team, you and I. A great team. I was thinking about the election coming up and--"

"Say Rich... I mean Mr. President," I interrupted, not wanting to hear what was coming next. I'd had a sudden brainstorm.

"Oh don't stand on ceremony Hank, what is it?"

"After this gets wrapped, I need to head to Lakota Nation to make some diplomatic contacts there. They're building a heavy presence in Mexico and I think it would be good to get to know them on their own ground. Sight 'em out before I meet 'em head on in Mexico."

"Good thinkin' Hank. I'll put a call in to John Blacknight and fix it up. They don't like us too much but they're suckers for an overture of friendship. That's how we'll beat 'em Hank. You remember that."

"Yes sir. Thank you sir." I almost choked on my own words.

"Bye Hank. See you when you get back from Lakota."

"See you then, Mr. President." I rang off and stared at the floor. I didn't ever intend to return to Texas. My best intentions to make this hellhole of a government respectable, got twisted at every opportunity. The twisted withered old oilman in the statehouse, watching over the Republic to make sure it moved steadily outward at all costs.

Kandel tapped me on the shoulder. "Sorry, didn't mean to interrupt. Do you have a minute?"

"Sure."

"You ok?" Kandel looked concerned.

"I will be."

"Well, I've got something I hope you can give me a hand on. A couple of vacationers from Las Cruces got caught over in Benson, Arizona and want to drive back but I'm afraid they'll get picked up. Especially with all the confusion over the border change."

"We'll need to have them checked at the border, they'll need full ID, proof of residence... oh fuck it. I'll give 'em my personal assurance. No questions asked. Just give me their plate numbers and I'll take care of the rest."

"They'll actually be in an ambulance when they go. One of them is pretty bad off. He got hit in Lordsburg." Kandel stared at me piercingly.

"Ah, hell give me their names. I'll tell the army he was hit by y'all and he's a hero with a Purple Heart coming to him. He won't have any trouble at all for the rest of his life."

Kandel wrote down the information.

"Thanks Hank. I'll be seeing you again."

"Don't count on it. " I turned and left.

STEVE - 12

Benson, Arizona

I lurked in the back of the small room and watched Simone kneeling at Sam's bedside, rubbing his head.

"You're gonna be fine baby." Simone fought back tears.

"Yeah. I have a firm belief that Sammy Davis Jr. will meet me at the pearly gates," Sam whispered softly.

They all laughed in spite of themselves.

"Don't talk that way honey. You just think positive and you'll be fine. The doctor says you're almost through the worst. And goddamn it, I won't let them take you away without taking me first." A tear traced down Simone's cheek.

Sam reached up and took the tear from her face and put his finger to his lips.

"I'm sorry, Simone. That's the first time I've ever made you cry. I won't do it again. I promise." A shudder passed through Sam.

"Hey, man," I said shakily. "We've got a gig together to do yet. Once all this shit is over. My Frank Sinatra to your Sammy. In Vegas. Dig."

"I dig, brother." A pale imitation of the smirk he used when imitating Sammy Davis Jr. played on his face. "Wouldn't miss it, Frank babe."

The smirk turned into a grimace and he closed his eyes hard.

"What's wrong Sam?" said Simone harshly.

"Nothing." His voice betrayed him.

"Now cut that shit out Sam. What's the matter?"

"I don't know." He jerked with pain again. "I think... Simone... baby... I love you... and..."

His face relaxed and the heart monitor went dead.

"DAMMIT!" screamed Simone.

Helen rushed out the door, yelling for the doctor. We backed off, as the doctor and nurses rushed in and tried to bring Sam's heart back.

The doctor shouted out orders as the nurses went to work. "Not too hard with the plate Sarah. He's all messed up in there. Just take it easy."

A slow heartbeat started up and Simone bit her lip. Tears streamed down her face. She stepped forward but the nurses nudged her back. Sam opened his eyes again and looked at Simone. He held her gaze and a tear streamed down his face, his mouth forming silent words, then his eyes closed. The heartbeat flatlined again and the doctors continued trying to jump-start his heart. Simone was bawling uncontrollably now. The doctors continued working for another five minutes. Finally, they stopped and turned to the group.

"I'm afraid he's gone."

Simone's crying diminsihed and she turned around. She looked at the floor and said softly, "I'm sorry Sammy. I'm sorry," then collapsed. I caught her before she hit the floor and held her. I waved off a nurse.

"Let her rest," I said. The nurse began to protest. "Let her rest I said! It's the best thing that could happen to her."

I picked her up and carried her back to the room. Mulu and Helen walked arm in arm, crying, behind me.

When Simone woke, she remained silent for a few minutes staring at the wall.

"I just feel like I've been robbed. Like I missed the big chance. I... shit. I can't think of anything but cliches right now. Some poet I am Sammy. Some goddamned poet." She began to cry again.

I held her and she rested against me.

Mark called at around 2 o'clock.

"Mark. I've got some really bad news. Sam didn't make it.... That's right.... I don't know. I think we should let that lie for right now. We'll figure it out later.... Uh-huh.... Right.... That doesn't matter.... What? Jesus, really? Whatever.... When.... Ok. We'll be ready.... That's fine. We won't have any trouble getting back out of there will we.... Right.... We won't.... Ok.... Thanks.... I will.... Bye."

I turned back to the group.

"Here's the deal. Me, Helen and Mulu are going to be let go, because we're Texans fleeing from political oppression. Simone has the choice of waiting for the settlement and then trying to get out some other way or just heading back to Las Cruces now. The Texans don't even know we're together, so there won't be any trouble either way. At this point they could care less. Mulu, you are of course free to go back to Denton."

"I don't think so."

"And Simone. I don't know how this will make you feel but Mark told the Texans Sam was wounded in action in Lordsburg and they want to give him a civilian purple heart. He'd go back as.... He would've gone back as a war hero."

She laughed morbidly. "He would've hated that. Oh shit, I don't want to talk about him in the past tense. He probably still hates it, don't you hon. Ummm. I have to go back. I can't take racing around right now. I want to go back and take care of Sam's stuff and... I need to see my dog. Now more than ever. She's all I've got."

I looked at her sadly. I wanted to go with her. To help her. I couldn't.

"Well that's settled. When in a disintegrating US, do as the politicians do." A mixture of bitterness and resolve welled up within me.

"Helen, Mulu and I will go to the Benson airport and try to catch a flight. There's one to Champaign through Chicago. The flight has been approved but they'll have to wait a while to be cleared for take-off. There can't be any military planes in the air when it leaves. That's part of the agreement. When we get to Chicago we can't leave the airport. If we do, we'll be stuck in Chicago and under who knows what jurisdiction. Simone can leave for Cruces as soon as the border is settled, which is what they're doing right now."

"What are you going to do in Illinois?" Helen turned to Mulu.

"Oh I'll find something to do." He looked nowhere in particular, as if the question embarrassed him. "They have a University in Champaign, right? I'm sure I could get something connected with that."

I interrupted, "I'm sorry Simone but we'll have to get packed and get going pretty soon here. When Mark gets back he'll talk to you about Sam. Helen, Mulu and I have to hurry up and wait. Once you get things figured out, you need to go down to the Benson outpost on the highway and await clearance. We're going to the airport."

Everyone got their bags together and trundled downstairs. Simone followed to say goodbye.

"I'll miss you. Be careful." Simone hugged me. Then checking to see that Helen was busy with her bags, she kissed me deeply, began to cry and turned away.

"I never knew how much I loved him." Her voice cracked hoarsely through her grief. She went back inside without waiting to watch the car go. She had to get back to Sam, lying coldly inside. She needed to get back to Las Cruces and bury him and burn his things and cry until the moon burned her tears away.

"Just the three of us." Helen looked intently at me.

"Yeah, the three of us." I sighed.

KOLBRASKI - 7
Arkansas

The bird which delivered me from danger, soon betrayed me and dropped me in a field somewhere in Arkansas. I walked the lonely road, hoping for some sort of reprieve. I would not lose faith. I just needed to wait for the next break.

Eventually, I heard a vehicle moving down the road from behind me. I felt it was a sign that I was on the right road. It was full of Ozark Mountain Troops. I flagged it down and asked for the commanding officer.

"That's me. What do you want, vag?" A tall burly man with thinning hair looked at me with the skepticism of the unsaved.

"Just a ride to the nearest encampment to rejoin the forces sir." I spoke cheerily.

"Vags don't ride on O.M.A. trucks, bud. Sorry. Let's go."

"Wait!" I pulled out my ID. "That's me."

The officer grabbed it and looked me up and down. The transformation must have been more thorough than I thought.

"I don't know where you got this buster but it's a high crime to steal an army man's ID,ok? I'm keeping this and we'll be on the look out for you. Drive!"

The truck took off and left me in the roadside dust. I began to understand the scene. My old self was dead. I'd been reborn. A new body and a new spirit. By taking the ID, the officer had symbolically liberated me of the last vestiges of my sinful self. I was a new man, nameless and free like the lilies of the field. I walked for awhile longer, hardly attending to my steps. Then the sign that I had mistakenly anticipated in the truck appeared. A little village set before me. Humble in its trappings and quiet. The sign read, 'Mount Judea--Pop. 20'

A man in overalls and an old hat came up the road towards me, carrying a shotgun loosely by his side. "Who are you?"

"I have no name, good sir. I am born again and anew under the light of God."

"You're that son of a bitch that crashed that hellycopter in muh field arencha? How in God's name did you live? That thing slammed right into the side of the mountain."

"Yes the bird did fail me but God doesn't and yet here I stand, fresh born and unrecognized to the world."

"You some kind of preacher?"

"Surely as you are, am I. I come to fight the Texans. Resist. We will win the day with fists of righteousness. God has shown me that the Ozarkians are the old way and unfit. But here in lovely Judea, the Promised Land anew, I will show thee how to fight the good fight."

"Yuh got bonked on your head good, that's fur sure. Why don't you come back to the house with me and we'll fix you up somethin' to eat."

"A fine show of charity sir, I will follow."

The honest man led me back to his humble palace, slightly adorned but rich in the grace of God and bid his wife put forth a feast.

"Ma! That guy that crashed the copter's alive. You wanna nuke him a couple pork sausages and some broccoli!"

With speed unaccountable, the good woman produced delectable morsels in front of me.

"I thank you ma'am. You are a good Christian woman, the likes of which I haven't seen in many a year. I give thanks to God for you, your husband, this shelter and this repast." I made a show of enjoying the food, smiling and looking at her with each bite so she had no doubt of my appreciation.

She stared at me with the eyes of a child. "Yew a preacher?"

"In that I be a servant of God, as all, I'll answer yes."

Joy drenched her plain face. "Why, our preacher took off with Kreena's daughter last year. We ain't had no preacher since. There's a church around the corner for you an' everything. Well it'd be quite nice to have a preacher again, though Pa'd probably disagree. Oh he's a good soul but gits a bit heavy under the lids on Sunday morning."

The man scorned the woman's words. "I don't know what kind a preacher you are son. But aside from what Ma here says about it, I'd sure like to have some Sunday guidance back in town. The church is all yours, seein's that I'm the Mayor anyways."

"I thought myself not fit to lead." Their offer alighted on my soul like a dove from heaven. "But I hear your call too well. Where is this house of God, that we may forthwith begin our mission? The First Church of Resistance. The first, I say, of many, which will multiply like a multitude and fight the evil Texas Satans with the power of God and truth, which will set us free."

"You got your preachin' things?" The woman arched her eyebrows.

"Uh... no."

"Lost in the crash, I expect," the man offered.

"Quite right, dear fellow, quite right. Much was lost in the crash."

"Well, no matter," the lady gave in. "You can borrow our bible and whatever else you need, until you get back on your feet."

"Thank you dear lady and sir. You are too kind."

"What's your name?" The woman eyed me curiously.

"You may call me Augustine Arisen." I glowed in the power of my new life.

"Well, Reverend Rizen, let's get yeh set up in your church."

HANK - 4
Pierre, Lakota Nation

I lit another cigarette. I never smoked. What was wrong with me? I'll tell you bucko. You're running from everything and not toward anything.

I'd made my perfunctory visit to the Lakota Nation Statehouse and met John Blacknight. He was cordial but not friendly. Then I booked a flight. The next one. It was to Missoula, Montana. From there I could cover my tracks through Chicago and get to Denver, where I could hole up with Croslin until I figured out what to do.

My God, what a phony I'd become. Selling out my people in Texas, selling out the New Mexicans and then running like a baby. What could I do to help? I'd been stuck in this cycle ever since I met Morgan on Mt. Bonnell. I wanted to blame it all on him but I knew I had given in every step of the way.

And I now I ran like a cur. If Morgan caught me, it'd be the end and if the US caught me, they'd come up with their own version of justice for me. Treason at every turn. I grabbed my bag and headed down to get a taxi.

"Donate money to help relieve the Libyans sir?" said a man who looked like a scrubbed up bum.

I seared him with a dirty look. "Whatever happened to bums who wanted spare change to buy a beer?"

"Well if you don't want to help, man just say so."

The man began to walk away.

"I wanna help!" I yelled after him. "How can I? Why the hell have I been put on Earth? To be tortured? Damned if I do. Ahhhh," I realized I was screaming in the street at no one.

I felt a hand touch my shoulder.

"Can I help you?" The voice came from a tall Sioux in flannel.

"No. I'm fine, just having a 7th or 8th mid-life crisis."

"So I see. You are a man from Texas."

It wasn't a question, it felt more like a diagnosis. Put that way, it made me feel a lot better.

"Yeah, and it's a frustrating place to be."

"It seems to me you're not there. Maybe you should have left your frustration there. But then frustration is like gum on your shoe."

"Who are you?" I backed away. He seemed to get a little too

personal too quick.

"Highway Security Marshall Eagle. I meant only to help. May I give you some advice? You don't have to listen and I won't tell you if you don't want to hear."

"All right I'm listening." I suddenly felt like the caricature of a blustery Texas cowboy getting wisdom from the aged chieftain in a spaghetti western.

"Book your flight through Lakotair if you want the freedom to travel."

I chuckled. "I thought it would be more mystical than a commercial recommendation. Like the winds that always blow and the rivers that run and stuff."

He didn't grin and kept a steady eye on me. "I know you wouldn't listen to that. I want to help, so I tell you what you are able to hear and understand."

"Well you're sure wise and helpful for a cop."

"To protect and to serve." A smile broke the seriousness of his countenance. "Now Hank Connely. Go get your flight. Remember that troubles always follow us. Sometimes the trick is choosing the right ones."

Before I realized he shouldn't know my name, he was off down the street and around the corner. Out of nowhere a huge bird swooped down low in front of me. I stumbled and almost fell as it screeched in my ear.

"Hey, man, you drunk?"

It was a taxi driver.

"I'm not gonna take you if you're drunk. We gotta call Freewheels for that."

I looked again and the street was empty. "No I'm fine. Take me to the airport please."

GEHRIG - 3
New York City

I had never been to New York and was overcome by the glass, steel and technology. If the Ozarkians hadn't paid my way, I doubt I ever would have come here at all. The capital of the United Nations had not lost its luster over its hundreds of years of existence. I took one of the museum-like subways to Rockefeller Center where Miss Condry had an office. I felt under-dressed wearing a suit in the cavernous elevator operated by an attendant. I got off at floor 23, went into Miss Condry's palatial office and announced myself.

The receptionist paused to speak something into a receiver around his neck and looked up. "Miss Condry will be right with you sir."

I nodded and kept looking around the outer office of Avon Information Inc.

"If you'd like to have a seat..." The receptionist waved a lithe hand towards a sofa that looked like it was made of bread boards.

"No thanks, I'll stand."

I walked over to a plaque that had a newspaper story emblazoned on it. It told about Miss Condry's work in finding singing star Al Crocetti's wife. Since that time, Miss Condry had made a hobby of finding missing persons. She was well connected, especially throughout the South. While she had no particular sympathies for the Ozarkians, she had agreed to take my case because she admired the book I had written, 'Handguns and the American Smile'. She thought it unfortunate that I had been sent into action only days after being roped into the army.

"Mr. Gehrig?"

I turned to see a woman with big hair, a white blouse, black skirt and red sparkling shoes, standing in a doorway.

"Come on in." She smiled sweetly. "I've done some preliminary checks, have a seat, some preliminary checks and I can't find anything on a Kolbraski. The only thing I've got is a lead on the 55th Texas regiment, which took a group of Ozarkian prisoners into battle near New Orleans. The only reason we've got anything on them is they came up against Marlowe's regiment and the prisoners apparently scattered causing a melee. Is that how you say that? Anyway, it was a big mess and one of the more famous altercations in the Louisiana invasion. Sort of made Mr. Marlowe's reputation. He's cleaning up on talk shows down there but goddamned Bantam got his rights."

I tried to hide my bewilderment with a blank look.

"To his book, Mr. Gehrig. Rights to his book. Anyway, the prisoners got scattered and ended up all over the bayou and who knows where. Some of them may have hitched deep into Alabama by now or caught rides from the Tuscaloosa boys when they went back. Now I'd do this myself if I wasn't so busy, but Avon'll bankroll you if you want to go down to Alabama and meet with Marlowe. He won't know anything for sure but he'll be able to put you on the right track. Whaddaya say?"

"It's the best thing I've heard so far."

"All right, then here's two tickets out of La Guardia to Tuscaloosa. Since we yanked our Senators out, you can't fly anywhere in the US because they're being buttheads, so we booked you through Philadelphia, which is apparently somebody's idea of the new capital. If anyone asks who you're loyal to, say something about the patriotic and you'll be fine. They don't care where you're from, because they're pretending none of this is happening. Just don't say anything about Washington, Columbia. Hell, just don't use the word Washington at all. Makes them nervous."

I took the tickets and thanked Miss Condry.

"Oh, and one last thing. Tell Jeb 'hi', and I'm going to get his next book." She smiled big and all but pushed me out the front door.

JEFF - 7
Missoula, Montana

Faye and I sat in a small hotel on Higgins Ave. in Missoula. I was trying to get through to Professor Croslin in Denver.

"No. Professor Croslin,.... Yes! Yes I'll... shit. Disconnected."

Faye looked up from her reading. "It sounds bad."

"Yeah it does."

"Don't worry, honey." Faye stroked my hair. "I'm sure he's ok. It's probably just miscommunication."

"Yeah you're probably right."

"Wait, you're upset AND you're agreeing with me. Are you going to be all right?" She was only half kidding.

"It's not so much that I feel I'm responsible. It's just that I'm not there. I'm stuck here and we can't get anywhere close to Denver. My story is useless until we can get out of here. I'm just... I don't know."

"Maybe if you went back to the Deskset lounge and worked on your stuff, it would help keep your mind off it."

"No. It would just make me think about it more. Let's go back to the airport and check one more time."

"Oh-h, ok, I guess it can't hurt." Faye was trying hard to be optimistic.

We caught a cab and wandered up to the airport information desk for the millionth time.

The attendant looked haggard but was patient. "No, I'm sorry no new information."

"Let's sit down for a minute, I'm wrecked, you know." I sat. We watched the other troubled passengers scurrying around trying to get planes and get places. I thought how fresh and exciting it had all seemed when we were in the Lakota Nation. Now I longed for easy travel and national security.

"Am I getting old?"

Faye looked at me oddly. "What...are you talking about?"

"I should embrace all this excitement but it just seems to get me down. Why do I miss the old rotten government?"

"Easy." Faye smiled. "Because you never got your plane hijacked, your projects rarely got delayed and your home never got invaded."

"So what does that say? Was it really better?"

"Hmmm, maybe in a lot of ways. But whenever anything is born, there's always pain and trouble. It remains to be seen. There are a whole lot of good things coming out of this. Don't forget what we saw in Lakota Nation."

"Yeah. You're right. This is just change, that's all. We'll get used to it. Everyone always complained about how boring and perverted our society was and now its shaken itself up in a big way. We'll have to see what happens.... Thanks. I feel much better. I knew there was a reason I tolerated you." I leaned towards her. She punched me gently in the ribs and we engaged in a long kiss.

"Excuse me," shouted a flight attendant striding over to us. "Are you two looking to get back to Colorado?"

We nodded our heads like spring loaded baby dolls.

"Well, we've got one flight running Missoula-Chicago-Denver right now. It's cleared for air flight by Texas, so there'll be no problem getting it there.

"It's probably a plane of Texan spies." I felt giddy.

"Je-ef!" Faye poked me in the ribs and turned to the attendant with a serious expression. "We would love to get on that flight. What can we do?"

The attendant smiled. "It's ok. I know you guys are tired. Follow me."

Within thirty minutes, we were on board USAir flight 667 to the Newcity of Chicago. We slept soundly to the lull of the engines. When I woke up, I looked out the window and saw the Mississippi River. I imagined I saw the St. Louis arch in the distance. I must have been hallucinating because St. Louis was too far south on the river for us to be headed to Chicago.

I turned and saw Faye had an odd look on her face. I opened my mouth to ask her about it, when the speakers crackled to life.

"Attention Ladies and Gentlemen. Please remain calm."

I just kept looking out the window giggling. I couldn't help it. It was too ridiculous.

"USAir is under the jurisdiction of the United States of America. The United States government has diverted our plane to land in Asheville, North Carolina. Due to reasons of national security, we cannot tell you any more information. However, USAir will provide compensation for the inconvenience in the form of flight vouchers and free accommodations in Asheville. We apologize greatly for the inconvenience."

Faye looked around. "Did you notice all the US Army personnel on this flight when we left Missoula? They're not in uniform but you can tell their Army. Look at the insignia on that computer. And the documents that woman's shuffling."

I reached forward and tapped the man sitting in front of me, who looked military.

"Are you in the US Army?"

"I'm sorry. I really can't tell you anything about the diversion." He began to turn back around.

"Well the diversion is obvious. We were just wondering why you were in Missoula. I thought everybody was in the Montana Alliance there."

The man turned back looking annoyed. "The diversion is obvious, huh? Talk like that'll get you time son."

Faye jumped in, "We just mean it's obvious there's something the military needs to do there. I mean, let's face it, anyone can put that together on this plane, and it really doesn't compromise your security any since we're all going to Asheville. We were just curious about Montana. But if you can't tell us, we understand. We're not reporters or anything. We're just nosy Nellys." Faye gave a big grin. She killed me sometimes with her ability to disarm anyone.

The man smiled. "Well, most of the Guard out in Montana did go over to the defense alliance. I mean, you know there's no regular Army troops anywhere in the US except on the Eastern Seaboard and abroad. But there were a few of us in the Guard, who'd been transferred to Montana or who'd been dying to get out, that didn't take the Montana oath. So they were shipping us through Chicago, back to Washington, for reassignment. That destination has been changed to Asheville."

Faye smiled at him.

"Ok, you're right ma'am. I don't even know why we're going to Asheville. But there are things I've heard that give me a good idea."

"Are we going to be in danger?" I realized how stupid it sounded.

"I can't answer that son." I bristled at being called son. "You two just follow the airline's directions and you'll be fine."

With that the man turned back around.

Then I got tapped from behind. Geez, what now? A middle-aged man in a suit leaned up. "Did you get anything out of him?"

I noticed a slight Texas accent. "Not really. Just that they're former guard troops getting shipped back east to join the US Army."

"Damn!" the man looked scared.

"What's wrong?"

"I'm trying to get to Denver to see a friend but I just can't seem to get there."

Faye's ears perked up. "Wow! We're trying to get to Denver too. We were coming from Pierre. Where were you coming from?"

The man looked furtive and whispered, "Originally? Nogales."

"Mexico?"

"Yes. Please don't spread it around."

"Are you.... Can you talk about it? I mean we're definitely not spies of any sort. I'm a student at the University of Denver and Faye here..."

"Hi, I'm Faye." She let social graces take over.

"And I'm Jeff. Jeff Conroy."

The man's face fell in surprise. "You're Jeff Conroy? You went up to the Lakota Nation to photograph it."

"Yes..."

"I was trying to get to Denver, to meet Jack Croslin, your professor. He tried to get me to come up earlier before I.... Before the state seceded. I would've gone on the trip instead of you." He looked at Faye.

"Are you the Congressman?" I recalled vague mentions of Croslin's friend in Texas.

"Yes.... My name's Hank Connely."

"So have you defected from Texas?" Faye blurted out.

"Shhh. Not so loud. The Texas intelligence network is pretty vast. When Rich Morgan finds out I'm gone, he'll raise hell and oil to get me back. I got assigned to the Diplomatic Station in Mexico City but before I could get there, the New Mexico thing broke out, so I headed to Nogales. After that, I realized a lot of things. I hopped a plane to Lakota Nation, ostensibly to make a brief diplomatic meeting before I flew to Mexico City. Instead, I hopped the next plane I could, which happened to be headed to Missoula. Meanwhile, my country's army is shooting at planes and, well, you know the rest."

I got excited. I wanted to know more. "What are you going to do when we get to Asheville?"

"Stay quiet and get on the plane to Chicago. At least I'll be safe at O'Hare. They don't let anybody but AAF troops arrest anyone there and I have no quarrel with the AAF."

"Well, if you need any help..." offered Faye meekly.

"Sure. Sure. Maybe we can all stick together right up to Jack Croslin's office."

STEVE - 13
Benson, Arizona

"We may finally get a break," I said coming up to Mulu and Helen. They were both laughing about something and didn't hear or notice me. "I said they're going to shoot us."

"Huh?" Mulu hadn't heard.

"What?" Helen turned serious.

"I said we may have got a break. But no one paid any attention, so I tried to say something to get your attention."

"What break?" Helen tried to smile.

"They've just approved a flight to Chicago non-stop. That means no trouble with occupied airports or anything like that. They just flew in a special jet. Kandel approved the flight himself and requested we be bumped to top priority. They'll announce the manifest in awhile now."

"Cool, so we'll like, be able to get out of this hellhole." Helen grinned.

"Yeah, cool." I tried to freeze her with a look.

Mulu looked uncomfortable. "I'm gonna go to the bathroom."

I watched him go. "He seemed happy. Well at least until I walked up anyway."

"Oh Steve stop it. I don't get all crazy when you and Simone are all happy to see each other. We're just trying to make the best of this crappy shit hole we're stuck in." She waved her arms at the airport around them.

"I don't know. I guess I'm just tired. You do still love me don't you?"

"Of course. Come here." She patted the space next to her.

I sat down and she began to rub my head. "When's the flight manifest come out?"

"Any time now." I felt very comfortable now but I didn't trust it. "I'll go check in a minute."

"I'll do it." Suddenly her hand jerked away from my head and I saw Mulu walking up.

"Hey Mulu, let's go check and see if the list is up yet." Helen patted me on the head. "You just stay here and rest."

They came back with the good news that we were all indeed on the list. Mulu went off to buy pizza for all of us.

As I watched him go, my jealousy got the better of me. "Why are you so fixated on Mulu?"

"Listen, Steve, will you drop it? I'm tired of talking about it. Maybe I'm spending more time with him than you, because all you do since Simone left is criticize me and make me feel bad for hanging out with Mulu. I mean Jesus, Steve, we're stuck in a war zone. There aren't any other people to hang out with."

"There's me."

"UHhhhgghhh. That's exactly what I mean. You just can't get off it can you?" She stared angrily off in the distance.

I stood. "I'm going to take a walk."

I stormed off to the main concourse. Concourse hell, I thought. This is three hangers with a hallway. I moseyed along, looking at the shop windows, trying to figure out Helen. It wasn't so much that she was in love with someone else. She wasn't any fun. She was like the US Government, I thought, smiling. She just kept on pushing and taxing and not doing anything good until the nation split apart. I stopped. And I had to keep pushing my borders out to protect myself. I looked up at the gate marked with a flight to El Paso, leaving in ten minutes. It was the only way to ensure my safety. Keep the borders far from the heartland to provide a buffer. It made sense now.

I walked back around to our seats and couldn't believe my eyes. In the full daylight in front of everyone, Mulu and Helen were kissing and they meant it.

"Hi."

"Oh my God." Helen jerked away panicked.

"Uhh, Steve." Mulu looked pained.

"Coulda guessed." I smiled unpleasantly.

"Steve. We're just not getting along and I don't know what I want. Everything's up in the air. I'm sorry you had to see this but it doesn't have to mean the end. We'll figure it out in Illinois."

"No. That's ok. You two have fun. I think I'll pop in on Simone." I turned on my heels.

"Steve! Where are you going? Steve!" Helen yelled after me trying to force her martial law down my throat. But I was seceding from this union. Time to expand my borders and protect my own heartland.

I walked up to the El Paso gate and bought a one way ticket on the spot. I got on and sat down next to an elderly German businessman. He spoke with only a hint of an accent.

"Otto Bauderbush." He introduced himself. "I work in plastics for the Texas National Air Defense. And you?"

"Well, I used to work in a book store in Austin but I got dragged out to New Mexico by some people and now I'm trying to get back."

"Why did you go to Arizona?"

"Following a girl."

"Ah." He nodded understandingly. "And now you have come to your senses, eh?"

I pursed my lips and thought for a second. "Yeah, I guess so."

"You seem like a bright young man. Are you German by descent?"

"Well, my Grandfather came over from Westphalia."

"Ah good. Good. Have you always worked in a bookstore? Or do you have another trade. A writer perhaps?"

"A good guess. I had a Journalism degree but never used it."

"And you have no job to return to?"

"Not unless the bookstore will take me back."

"What would you say if I were to give you a job? Hmm?"

"I don't know anything about plastics. Besides, I'm going to Las Cruces to see a friend."

"Another girl, hmm? Very well. But the job I have for you is in Las Cruces."

"Oh yeah?"

"Yes. With the Texas Department of Propaganda. We need a writer. Someone with a journalism degree."

"Uh.. yeah. I don't know if I could work for the government."

"Why not? You are from Texas, right?"

"Well, yes.

"You are bright and can do the job. I can see that. You do not approve of the wars maybe?"

"Well that's not it really. Lately I've come to appreciate the principle behind putting up a good defensive space around you. It keeps you from getting hurt."

"Very astute. And true. So what, then, is the problem with working for the state?"

"I don't know. To be honest, I never have liked Texas much."

"When you lived in Austin, you did not like it. Perhaps the elements of disaffection there, permeated you. But now you see, you yourself are returning to Texas. It is not so bad is it?"

"Well, no. My outlook has changed a lot. I always felt like the Texans were after me and going to come get me."

The man chuckled. "And did they?"

"No."

He pointed a finger. "Even when you fled with this girl to Arizona?"

"No. In fact they gave us safe passage back and were going to award my friend medals before he died."

"I am sorry about your friend. But you see, your hate has been personal, towards your situation. Perhaps Austin. Perhaps the girl. But now you are freed and you see, the hate is not against Texas but against yourself for living a lie. Come work for us and you can help others to see the truth."

A warm feeling of acceptance came over me. I found myself in the right place with people who understood me. "All right, I will. I'll give it a shot."

The man winked and patted me on the shoulder kindly. "Very good. You are a smart man."

GEHRIG - 4
Tuscaloosa, Alabama

"Mr. Marlowe is always at the bar on Friday night. Can I help you?" The casually dressed soldier looked earnest and neutral.

I explained my mission, mentioning Ms. Condry's name and the guard offered to have someone drive me over to the bar.

The bar was called Marlowe's, and was a small hole in the wall near the college. Captain Marlowe stood behind the bar, tending it. The bar itself was at the very back of the building facing the front door. Tables and chairs littered the rest of the floor in no particular order. The driver went up to Marlowe and explained the situation as I sat down on a stool.

The legendary southern leader came over with a sly grin and shook hands with me. "I hear your buddies got caught in some crossfire."

"Yes, I was hoping you could help me. Miss Condry said they might have been--"

Jeb stopped me with an upheld hand. "Names and descriptions please."

"Uh, you want their names and.... Ok... uh, Mack Kolbraski is the first. He's sort of well, hairy, like a lot of facial hair. It keeps growing so fast, he can't shave it off and his hair is curly, not like mine but sort of wild and he's about 5' 9" but strong and he's Polish and--"

Marlowe interrupted me and pointed at his temple. "He have a vein right here on his temple and kind of a high forehead?"

"Yeah, and--"

"Yep, he was there and the other guy was balding, slightly rotund reddish, complexion and Irish if I'm not mistaken."

I know I must have looked stunned. "Yeah, that's John."

"Kolbraski's dead. Mcgillicutty is in Asheville."

Now I definitely looked stunned. "What?"

"Yeah, I met a few of the prisoners in New Orleans after the battle and did what I could for them which wasn't much at the time. Before we could get Kolbraski set up, he went out for a walk and was last seen going off with an operative from an underground drug league called The Robes. They take hard luck cases and send them on suicide drug delivery missions. If Kolbraski went on one of the missions, he was killed upon delivery. If he refused, he was killed on the spot. That's the way they work. I'm sorry."

I couldn't think of a thing to say. I felt fully responsible and yet couldn't comprehend it as real.

Marlowe seemed indifferent. He lit a cigarette and kept talking. "As far as Mcgillicutty goes, after we found out about Kolbraski, he caught a ride with me here and worked for a while, then took off for Asheville to try to get back to Illinois through Chicago. He's hoping to rejoin the Ozarkians in St. Louis."

I finally found my voice. "Well, darn. I have to get a plane to Asheville."

"Not tonight you don't." Marlowe spit on the floor behind the bar.

"Why not?"

"Dog lips sink ships. Just wait till tomorrow morning. You'll be fine. Keep tuned to a netcast at your hotel."

Jeb turned back and grabbed his beer. "Hey, Carney...." He walked over mumbling something to his friend. I got up and began to slump towards the door. I couldn't believe Kolby was dead. And in such a stupid way, after all he'd survived.

"Hey, uh... what's your name..." I heard someone behind me say.

"Gehrig," yelled Marlowe.

"Hey, Gehrig," Carney came up and put a hand on my shoulder. "I just want to tell you that what you're doin' is just great. You'll do fine and you'll get your friend back. I'm sorry about your other friend. That ain't right. Don't mind Jeb. He's a surly bastard sometimes but he means well. Good luck." Carney raised his beer in a salute and returned to the bar.

I felt a little better. I turned around and joined them for another round.

JEFF - 8
Asheville, North Carolina

Hank, Faye and I deplaned and headed immediately for the ticket counter.

Hank was muttering with nervousness. "Goddamn, US patrolmen everywhere."

Faye tried to calm him. "Don't worry. We just want tickets."

He gave her a miserable hunted look. "But I've only got a Texas ID."

"My treat." I couldn't stand to see him torture himself. "You're all with me in Colorado. Poor Colorado, which is getting the hell beat out of it by Texas. Oh please kind sir, may I please get myself and my poor friends back to our home before it burns." I rubbed fake tears from my eyes.

"E-nough." commanded Faye.

We got in line behind a bedraggled, unshaven man.

I nudged Hank. "You obviously don't need a shower, so why an ID?"

"Stop." Faye hated it when I talked bad about others. "Who knows what he's been through."

Hank found hope. "Maybe he'll draw all the suspicion onto him and we'll get by."

"Don't place so much hope in the misfortune of others." Faye took a few steps forward with the line as if to distance herself from our ill-gotten hopes.

Hank stopped and gave her an odd look. She was right and he knew it. He had told us on the plane how he felt responsible for the war. Maybe it would have happened without him but he sure helped it along. And for what, in the end? To be running from the very thing he'd helped create? He felt horrible and Faye had just pierced him to the marrow without realizing it.

Faye leaned forward towards the dirty man. "I don't mean to pry but I was wondering where you're coming from. We're all coming from Montana trying to get back to Colorado."

The man looked tired and puzzled that anyone not in uniform would talk to him. "Illinois, I mean Texas."

Faye nodded sympathetically. "I see. So how'd you get here?"

The man looked around and raised his voice so the MPs could hear.

"I'm from Illinois but I was visiting Texas, and they took my ID and pressed me into service. They planted fake credentials on me to make me look like a war prisoner from Ozarkia. But I got away. I have no idea how I'm going to get tickets."

I started to offer help but the MPs were already on top of him. It seemed like a pretty dumb thing to say it so loud but I guess he knew what he was doing.

"Sir, we need to see your ID." One MP barked out orders while the other searched him and took out a wallet from the man's pocket.

"No money. No passport. Ozarkian ID. Platonic Republican. O.P.C. Infantryman First Class John A. Mcgillicutty." He slapped the wallet back into John's chest.

The first MP who was taller and had a mustache mocked him. "You care to sing us a resistance oath boy?"

"I was just telling these people here--" MP mustache cut John off with a slap.

"Traveling together are you. Fine. We caught your little conspiracy here. As of now, you and your two friends here are in the custody of the United States Army as suspected enemies of the state."

"No you don't!" shouted Hank. We turned, wide eyed. He confronted the MP with fire and confidence. The air of despair had disappeared.

"Ambassador Hank Connely of the Republic of Texas." Hank approached the MPs, badge in hand, making Faye and me cringe. "These two are Midwestern spies from Illinois, that have been aiding the riots in Arizona. I've been tracking them all over the country. The Republic demands they be remanded into Texan custody and extradited for trial."

"Are you serious?" The shorter MP stared at Hank.

"Damn straight I'm serious. Serious as the US debt is large. I'll take 'em back with me right now."

John looked at Hank with fiery hatred. "You Cretins!" he shouted. "You're a demented concept, full-blown into human form. All of you Texans. A flaw in reasoning turned virus and running rampant through humanity. You use ideas like clothing. Masters at quick change. You took our rights and forced us to kill for you and then thanked us with our murder. May you and your countrymen rot in the filth which you've created!"

Hank scoffed at John. "Of course he's lying. He was not pressed into service. But he is telling the truth that he is not from Ozarkia. He's a filthy Midwestern spy."

The MPs looked at each other. "Come on you." Mr. Mustache grabbed Hank. "We have a few questions, routine of course, that we ask all Texans who happen to wander through our paths."

"Hank," yelled Faye but I nudged her to be quiet.

"We've got to do something." I feared she'd try to run after Hank.

"Do you know him?" The MP turned on Faye.

Before I could stop her, Faye blurted out, "Yes! He's from Texas but he was trying to get away from them and start a new life."

By this time, the MP was checking our Colorado ID's.

"Pre-war." He tapped them against his wrist as if to confirm their authenticity. "Rarely fakes. Been away a while?" He seemed to become slightly friendly.

I answered before Faye's honesty got us in more trouble. "Yes, several months."

"Well folks, my advice to you is stay clear of these characters. As you can see, they're playin' you for sympathy one moment and showin' their real hand the next."

"As for you..." He turned on John who crumpled back down into submission. "Clean yourself up and get to a US ID station before you get in any more trouble," and with that, he walked off to join his mustachioed pal.

"I can't believe what just happened." Faye suffered severe justice frustration.

John cautiously stepped towards us. "You did know him then? He wasn't hunting you?"

"No he wasn't hunting us. We were helping each other." Faye turned slowly and found a vent for her anger. "And you know what mister. He just saved your fucking life. So save all that over-ideological metaphorically polluted bullshit for the real enemies. Ok? That man was turning around to face what he'd done and get out of Texas. Now who knows what punishment they'll give him? But he saved your life doing it! Do you understand?" She panted to catch her breath but seemed calmer.

John got quiet. "Yes. I understand. At least he's not in Texas."

"Who knows! They'll probably extradite him."

I tried to inject some balance. "No. The US isn't cooperating with Texas on anything. He'll stay here. But that's what I'm worried about. What they'll do to him as a Texan.

Faye's anger had transformed into restlessness. "Well, let's not just stand around let's do something."

"Faye, the best thing we can do is get tickets and get a motel room and call Croslin to tell him what happened." I continued my balancing act.

"I'm calling him right now." Faye strode off to find a quiet place to make a call.

"I'm sorry about that," John said. "I had no idea what was happening."

"It's ok." I looked worriedly off in the distance. "She's like this. Jumping to the rescue. Understandable for you to be tense in your situation. So you've been on the run from the Texans?"

"Yeah. All through the south."

"Well look, before she gets back let me offer to share a room with you. I know you need it, and honestly we could use the safety of numbers. I'm uneasy about the whole military thing here."

John fingered a scrap of his shirt that hung loose. "I'll... uh... need help with uh..."

I touched his shoulder reassuringly. "No problem. You're with me."

Faye had no luck reaching Croslin. When she got back, she agreed to share the motel room with John. In our travels, both of us had become good at spotting bad characters. As angry as she was about Hank, Faye could tell, as I could, that John's heart was in the right place.

I had no problem buying four tickets. The fact that the MP's had already confronted us all and let us go, eased the process. The ticket attendant didn't even ask for my ID. We left the airport to go get some sleep.

I woke up at six the next morning to what sounded like a parade. I walked out into the motel parking lot and heard cheers off in the distance.

"What's going on?" Faye rubbed the sleep from her eyes.

"I don't know. Must be a football game or something."

We headed back in to make coffee, not thinking twice about it, really.

"What's all that yelling?" John yawned wearily from the floor.

"There must be some kind of game or festival or something," I answered. "It's coming from off towards downtown."

John sat up and shook his head. "I thought I heard gunshots."

I listened close and could now discern what sounded like guns being fired amid the cheering.

Faye squinted uselessly out the dirty window. "Maybe it's firecrackers. It just sounds too good natured to be some kind of disturbance."

John held a hand carefully up to his head and laid back down. "I feel like a truck tire. The tread part, that gets blown off into the road. Not that I wish to appear ungrateful. Thank you very much for allowing me to use your floor to become a truck tire." He fell back down.

"Here's some coffee." Faye set it down by John's head. The aroma seemed to have some effect. I tuned the old beat up motel radio to an ABR station, to see if they would shed any light on the frat party going on outside.

"For American Unity Radio, I'm Greg Whitney. Before we begin the week in review George Halberstam has a special report from Asheville, North Carolina."

A crowd cheered loudly in the background of Halberstam's report.

"That is the sound of hundreds of people here in downtown Asheville, cheering the Bluegrass Army, which waltzed into Asheville today without firing a shot."

"Oh shit," said John.

"This scene is typical of the Bluegrass invasion that began last night in the western halves of Virginia, Maryland and North Carolina. The US Army has retreated to a position in the mountains. Things may get bloodier there, but for now the Bluegrass Army is enjoying easy victories and massive public support throughout the mountain communities."

Whitney asked, "George do you have any idea what prompted this invasion and what the Ken-Ten Alliance's goals might be?"

"Well Greg, the official word from Lexington is these counties called upon the Bluegrass Army for protection from US martial law. I seriously doubt there will be a fight when the Bluegrass Army meets the US troops. For American Unity Radio, I'm George Halberstam in Asheville, North Carolina."

"Thank you George. The Ken-Ten Alliance, now called the Bluegrass Republic, began marching its troops over the US border yesterday. We'll keep you posted on any further developments.

"Now, The Week In Review.

"Sunday, Mexico forced negotiations in Arizona. On Monday, California, Arizona, Mexico, Texas and several Native American groups, including the Apache Nation, signed a treaty ceding a safe zone to Mexico. Ironically, the zone corresponds roughly to the area of the Gadsden Purchase, which the US bought from Mexico by force in 1853. The treaty came too late to save some 4,000 dead in the fighting.

"West Virginia joined the Bluegrass Republic on Monday. The US Congress challenged the move but took no further action.

"Washington State requested Canadian protection and assistance on Wednesday. The state has been operating independently, without federal aid since the budget crisis. Canada has sent some military into Washington, to fight Aryan Nation insurgents there.

"The same day, Oregon declared sovereignty. The state said it will temporarily operate as a fully autonomous unit but remain part of the US.

"Also on Wednesday, the Bluegrass Republic and the Ozark People's Republic negotiated a peace. The Ozark Army left Memphis, to concentrate on the battles with Texas. The Ozarkians are satisfied that the Bluegrass Army will prevent the Texans from moving through Memphis."

There was a slight pause and then a woman's voice began to shout over the sounds of an intense battle.

"...however, we are going to stay on the air as long as possible. Once again, the Texans are in Golden, where our studios are but they have not reached any farther. Do not panic. The Colorado Guard is holding them steady here in Golden."

A sound like a roof caving in ripped across the speakers.

"Could be steadier, but all our reports show the Texans are not advancing... huh... we're just caught behind enemy lines.... Ok, let's get back to, uh--WHAT? SO WHAT? Ladies and gent..."

The broadcast ended in static.

"Oh my god!" Faye held her hand up to her mouth. I shook my head.

"The sound of local ABR newscaster Anna Lubov, as Texas troops reached Denver on Thursday. They faced little opposition in the western counties. Denver does not wish to become part of Texas and has stopped the Texan advance at Golden, Colorado.

"The UN office of terrorism and war, released facts and figures associated with the disturbances in the west and south. Damian Mortley puts them in perspective."

"People have loved to turn their backs on the fighting that threatens not only our continent but perhaps the entire world. Many do not realize they are turning their backs on people in need. The failure of the US government to mobilize the army and maintain order is not laughable. It is deadly sad. During the conflicts, one million people have been permanently or temporarily dislocated. 250,000 are known dead. 100,000 are missing. These were Americans. They were Jimmy Sweetwater of Texarkana, Arkansas, Maria Gomez of Wichita, Kansas and Holly Baker of Alexandria, Louisiana. They were many more and they died for what? Not for freedom, not for liberty. They died for a line; a border line, a budget line, a dotted line, but they died. How many more must follow them, before their corpses finally catch our notice and force our hands. The people must take action. Because it's the people... not Richard Morgan or President Crowell...who are dying. My eye is no longer on Washington, my eye is on YOU and the rest of North America. I'm Damian Mortley."

Greg Whitney's reassuring voice returned.

"The US claims the UN's statistical methodology is flawed.

"Thursday, the Pennsylvania legislature put forth a unique bill among the number of legislative maneuvers we've seen in the past few months. H.R. 11236 declares that the federal government has abandoned the constitution and asks all states to send delegates to Philadelphia for a constitutional convention. Washington officials laughed at the bill but the latest survey shows Pennsylvanians overwhelmingly support it. Counties in eastern Ohio announced they will choose delegates to send to Philadelphia. No other states have responded.

"Once again, the Ken-Ten Alliance, now called the Bluegrass Republic, invaded the western halves of Maryland, Virginia and North Carolina, Friday night. The US Army is stationed at the foot of the Appalachians and Alleghenies to halt the invasion."

Everyone looked at me as if I knew why this happened. I shrugged. "Well, I guess we should head down to the airport anyway." There was nothing else to do but see what trouble we'd get into next.

"Poor Anna. Jeff, I hope she's ok. She's so great. That would be awful if..." Faye trailed off.

"I can't say Anna's been in worse, Faye, but remember when she kicked that male supremacy activist in the balls on a national netcast? She'll take care of herself."

"I guess you're right. Boy, I'm excited about going home now." Faye put on an almost genuine smile. "Let's go to the airport kids!"

I tried to boost John into action. "Yeah, come on John. The sooner we get there the sooner we can get out of here, hopefully."

The Sun - 6

The sun cooked the Nation, searing the smoking land. Millions sweated in airports trying to get back to the places they'd been before the fighting began. In the hot crucible of this American summer, the country had changed forever.

Across the broken continent, in airports, cabs, and airplanes; in capitols and in cabins, the disparate peoples of a broken nation paused to hear one last plea from the country that was dying.

An older woman's voice began to speak.

"Ladies and Gentlemen, we stand at a dark time in our history as a nation. The trials and tests of the first Civil War are multiplied ten fold in this one. Some citizens have called for great wars to be fought. And some rebel states have decided that is the way. I think that it is not and I think the President is prudent to refrain from escalating the conflict through increased military actions. Domestic conflicts have been reasoned out at the UN bargaining table before and that is what must happen now, if we are to preserve this country whole, instead of in smoking ruins. I call on each and every one of you tonight, whether you are in a rebel territory or not, to call or write your elected representative and your Head of State and beseech them to end this madness. Only through negotiations will we avoid an utter catastrophe and holocaust. Our problems are not so divisive that we cannot resolve them without gunfire and bloodshed. Democracy and freedom will win the day. I believe that. And if you believe it too, then together, we can end this horror and plague in the great United States of America."

The world paused and then Jack Deleo said, "Former President Jane Michael. Her administration was the last to operate with a surplus. This is American Unity Radio."

The sun set and the broken pieces of the land cooled somewhat by the venerable woman's speech. South Florida joined the Caribbean Alliance. The remains of Kansas, Nebraska and South Dakota became part of the Colorado Republic and helped to defend Denver from the Texans. The Bluegrass Republic negotiated a cease-fire with the US; and Canada put forth a resolution to hold peace talks in Vancouver.

JEFF - 9
Asheville, Bluegrass Republic

We pulled up to the Great Smokies Airport. Inside, everything had changed. The place crawled with Bluegrass Army patrols. John had no idea what to expect.

"All flights are canceled." I returned from the ticket counter shaking my head. "But they're trying to get everyone to New York or Chicago since those are the easiest airports to get into. I put us on a reserve list for Chicago. I don't know how long it'll be."

John looked scared again. He seemed in some ways like a beaten dog. "Any problems with me?"

"No, none at all, John. Faye just needs to be vaccinated before we board."

"Ha. Ha." She smacked me gently.

I stopped her with mock concern. "You think I'm juvenile don't you?"

"I think you're crazy." She put on her chicken voice and began poking me. When the rumble finished, we turned to John to apologize but he wasn't there. We found him over by the bar talking animatedly to a short man in a suit with slightly wavy brown hair, clutching a beer and sitting on a barstool grinning. He waved us over.

I took up the invitation. "I guess they know each other."

Faye followed. "Brilliant deduction."

"I hope you didn't drive here." John laughed as we got within earshot.

"Hey guys." John turned to us. "This is my friend, Gehrig, who's been chasing all over the high powered publishing industry and into the deep south looking for me. Gehrig this is Jeff Conroy and Faye..." he paused searching for a last name.

"Tull," said Faye.

John stared at her.

"No. I'm serious. My parents were dorks. I can't help it."

"Faye Tull." John enunciated distinctly. "Jeff is a photographer and Faye was helping him out on a shoot in the Lakota Nation."

"Pleasure to meet you." Gehrig shook our hands firmly. "So where are you guys headed now?"

John answered for us, obviously still overjoyed at seeing his friend. "Well, they're headed to Chicago, so I'm gonna tag along with them and try to fly into St. Louis from there. Wanna come?"

"Sure, why not?" Gehrig looked as if we might explain to him why not. "Too bad Steve and Helen aren't here. We could have a little University reunion."

Faye sensed the concern and tried to allay it. "We're headed back to Denver, if there's anything left of it. We haven't been able to get through on the phone for days."

"Well, if you don't mind me tagging along, I'll accompany you to Chicago." Gehrig looked somewhat hopeful that he had interpreted Faye correctly.

She didn't let him down. "Not at all. That'd be great."

"Cool, I'll put us on the next plane." His enthusiasm impressed me but I hardly believed him.

"Yeah, right Gehrig. We'll be sitting by the President too, huh?" John, slapped Gehrig a little roughly on the back.

"No man, I'm serious. Miss Condry gave her word of gold with the airport manager. As soon as the Bluegrass Army got here, I was told to get on whatever plane I wanted, with whomever I wanted."

John still looked skeptical. "How did you manage that?"

Gehrig got in John's face. "I told some sob story to a powerful publishing magnate about some schmo getting lost in Arkansas and she took pity on me. By the way, I get ten percent off the top of your memoirs." He grinned.

"Like Hell." John backed away and raised his voice.

"Like you can even write, Mcgillicutty." Gehrig backed off too.

"Old college pals huh?" I grinned.

"Yeah." John became suddenly somber. "You heard about Kolby, huh?"

He had told us the night before about his friend and commanding officer, Kolbraski, dying in a drug deal in New Orleans.

"Yeah," Gehrig hung his head and seemed to look ashamed. "That was hard. To go through all that and get snubbed out so randomly. But it's war time." Gehrig ironically cheered up. "There'll be time for crying when the shooting stops."

"You've been watching too many movies." John smirked.

"Who's getting you on that plane, Johnny boy?" Gehrig mussed John's hair. It was an incongruous sight.

I decided to stop feeling like an intruder and express some appreciation. "Thanks Gehrig, we really appreciate this."

"Sure. Let's just hope we don't get hijacked." He took a final swig of his beer. "I'll be right back." With that, he got up and walked through a door marked 'no admittance.'

"My little Gehrig is moving up in the world. But what do you expect from a criminology student. I just hope the plane doesn't crash into a wall." John looked at his beer. "To Mack." A tear rolled out of one eye. He took another big swig.

KOLBRASKI - 8
Mount Judea, Ozarkia

"This is my body. Take it and eat it. Do this in memory of me," I sermonized from the pulpit. A good 6 of the 20 inhabitants of New Judea had turned out to hear my sermon. Some of them looked a bit worried. I would rest their fears.

"I've never seen Holy Communion done with microwave sausages before." The woman who'd fed me my first night there piped up quite inappropriately.

"Quiet, madam. This is a solemn and holy service. The mysteries cannot be knownst to all but the initiates, else they would be but common aphorisms as gravel to swine. Now.

"Take this and chew it. This is my stubble, do this in memory of me."

Another woman impertinently interrupted. "I know our Lord and Saviour Jesus Christ didn't say anything about stubble nor with no broccoli neither."

"I'M saying it now, my dear lady." I shook my glowing mane which covered now almost every inch of earthly flesh about my face. She cowered back in the presence of my divine hairiness.

"The First Church of Resistance is not REformed but TRANSformed. We must all seek the true enlightenment of the truth that makes us holy. You see but bits of common everyday food here and scoff. But I ask you, what was more common in Jesus' day than bread and wine. What more common! Speak!"

The lady acknowledged her ignorance with tacit silence. Ah, the bliss of the unknowing.

"And so, to drive out the Texans, to excommunicate, excoriate and EXORCIZE them from this land, we take the common goods of our table, representing that first meal given to me by yonder good lady on the first day when God sent me unto this town, to begin his revolution."

The service went on after that without a hitch. No one spake a word but contemplated the mysteries of the sausage with simple divinity. I was well pleased with my new converts. I could see it writ on their faces they would be telling friends soon about this new church.

After the service, I retired to the rectory and had my manservant, Abe, fetch me some grapes, cool water and a fan.

"Grapes is no problem Gus..." Abe paused on the threshold of the veranda.

"That's Augustine Arisen, you... precious soul." I waved him on.

"But like I says Gustine Grizen, the grapes is no problem and the water ain't warm but why do you want a fan out here in the garden. You cain't even plug it in."

"Not that kind of fan, dear man. A fan like this." I made the sign of the dove with my hands. "Made from paper not from man-made steel."

Puzzled thought labored across Abe's face. "But isn't paper man-made?"

I smiled tolerantly. "Go Abe, and fetch them quick."

He left and just in time. The company I did not want the fool around for, arrived. Four men of able body had approached me one night and I revealed the plan for the secondary revolution. While the church blinded the Texans with the truth, the revolutionary crusaders of resistance would cut the legs out from under them.

"All we could find besides our shotguns, was this old pickaxe. All the other stuffs too big and heavy. It's all damned 'puter mechanized like my pap used t'always say." The noble leader Geoffrey presented their armory.

"Hell Jeff." His consultant added from the background. "Why don't we just get us some beer in town and grab a few more rifles while we're at't. Tain't no trouble and worth the trip I says."

"Well said and well met, gentleman," I approved of their plan, bolstering their spirits. "Here is the coin which you do require on your journey. I hope it does provide you something extra for your entertainment."

"Hey this is five bucks." One of the more scurvy squires complained. "This won't buy bubble gum, paps. Why donchoo keep it and buy a shave."

We all laughed at his mirth and I assured him, like Samson, I remained strong without the blade.

He ceded the truth of my words. "You does smell strong."

I soothed him with humble words of mirth. "What ho, gentle knight. You wound me. Now, to the task at hand and be quick, for the revolution cannot wait."

"C'mon let's just take the five bucks and beat it. We can at least get a beer with it."

"What! Are we gonna split it four ways?"

The men trailed off in their happy joyousness, boosting each other's spirits, to my enjoyment, to help them along their happy sun filled day. I lay back among the knotted pines of ol' Mount Judea, resting place of the divine and holy. The sun looked down on me kindly, warming me throughout like a maiden drawing water from a well. I felt the spirit rushing within me, ready to bring forth new wonders on the Earth. The revolution had begun. I thought of the happy worshipers that morning, in devout obeyance and how they would but multiply, spreading across the land like lots of tacks on a bulletin board. I envisioned the new revolutionary army, marching to arms, raising up the poor and weak behind them as they went, until they swelled their ranks to thousands strong.

I realized also, Abe had not returned with the fan and I was getting sore burned by the sun. I went inside to rest. How heavy lies the head that wears the crown.

KANDEL - 6
Tucson, Arizona

The Californians had finally ordered me back to Los Angeles. I'd receive my new assignment on the flight back, tomorrow. Stephanie had moved back to L.A. after they secured Nevada. Some friends hinted she'd taken up with someone new. Big surprise there, BUT... ahh, I didn't care anymore. I had plenty to worry about. I'd become a star in the California Republic. If anything, Stephanie needed me. Yeah.

I kicked a rock and watched the pink sunset below as I walked along a mountain ridge outside Tucson. Yeah, VIP in California, you damned killer. I had tried to do the right thing. I'd ended up responsible for the deaths of several thousand people, including Steve's friend Sam. The higher purposes the California Peace Party espoused, fell apart in the face of that. They could have left Arizona out of it. Then Texans would have rolled through the entire southwest. Who's to say it would have been worse? Still, people died at my feet, following my orders and I hadn't gotten too comfortable living with that yet. It was one thing to kill a man directly. It's another thing to order someone, or even a bunch of someones killed. It's even worse to send someone to their death. Who had I become? I looked at my red sun-scarred hands.

The trail wound around the mountain like a bright red ribbon. The sunset dimly lit the way ahead. I thought I saw someone sitting on the side of the trail. When I got there it turned out to be an old stump. I still hadn't gotten used to the heat out here. I'm a seaside man you know. This hot desert, no humidity stuff, plays havoc with my sensitive skin. I mean, I'm a sensitive guy, why else would I be blubbering on in my head, non-stop, about the wonderful job I'd done killing people.

I really regretted Stephanie being like that. Whoops jumped track. Happens. But she hadn't even dumped me. Just sent me to my death and strolled back to L.A. to pick up with someone else. Was she such a coward? She had to send me to a war zone to avoid confronting me?

I saw someone again in the dimming glow ahead. This time I was sure, so I approached slowly and found a pile of leaves, sticks and shrubs, wound around a clump of scrub brush. I took a big drag out of my water bottle. I hadn't been gone long enough to have heat sickness.

I still hadn't decided if I wanted to stay in California. I joined the CPP to change the US, not secede. Maybe I should move back to Illinois and hide out in a small town. Get a teaching position at the High School, like so many of my burned out friends. Would they let me go now anyway? Sure they would. They just wouldn't like it.

This time, when I saw someone ahead on the trail I ignored it. There are ways to beat back insanity, I've always figured. Just keep your head down and concentrate. People have told me I'm crazy for thinking that. Ironic, huh? The sun had almost set and it was impossible to distinguish the forms ahead. I turned around to head back to my car.

"Mark Kandel," whispered a hoarse unrecognizable voice.

Ok, time to breathe the fairy dust and face the leprechauns. If I'm gonna lose it, I'm at least gonna look it in the eye as it leaves. I turned and saw what I thought had been a rock, move and walk over to me. No drugs had been taken, I promise you.

"Who is it?" I roughly shouted, to cover my disquiet. That kind of thing just gives you away though.

"A friend," the voice croaked. "You worry. I've come to help you not worry." The form had gotten near enough for me to see an old man wrapped in many colored blankets, with depictions of hunts and battles and histories woven into them. The setting sun gave too little light for me to see the man's face.

"You honor the dead. Death has surrounded you too long. Do not flee death, let it flee you. If you try to run away, you will run into its arms. Death is part of life, Mark. It is no one's fault. No one should take life from another. But there is no stopping it in the end. Forget about your heartache. And return to the life you have helped make possible. Things are good in your land. Enjoy them. Spread them. Make them better. It is heat that brings change and life."

"That's great. Who the hell are you?"

The man began to walk past me into the woods. Right before he disappeared in the darkness he turned his face toward the last of the setting sun and, Dead Lenny Bruce as my witness, I swear I saw the dead Apache chief. A hawk chose that time to race up into the night sky and soar straight to heaven.

STEVE - 14
Las Cruces, New Texas

"But you're not the same Steve. I don't even know who you are."

Those tired words. Simone had built up a wall I couldn't surmount. It was a new thing in our relationship. I'd tried to explain the inner workings of Texas, to her benefit. How she could benefit from Sam's heroic death. She just didn't listen.

"How could I change overnight Simone. You think Helen and that bastard have screwed me up that much? Give me a break. I was just denying the real good of the state, because I was selfish. Look Simone. I'm sorry. This is no time to argue. You need support. There's a war widows' meeting every Saturday--"

"Steve, you know me don't you? I wouldn't go sit around with a bunch of old women spilling their guts. Publish it in a national magazine through a poem, yes, but..."

"Then submit something to New Texas, if it would make you feel better."

She grimaced. "I'd rather die than have my poem in that piece of trash."

"Watch what you say Simone. You don't mean that. C'mon I'm there for you--"

"Don't say that anymore Steve. You aren't you anymore. You're some Texas-mad drone. You let them take your mind because you couldn't deal with it anymore. Now go. And take your stupid offers and leave me alone until you get some sense again."

I left. She was angry. It was best to let it lie. She needed time to think and not mope. I had it. The propaganda office could suggest folks for mandatory rehab. It was often used for subversives and demagogues but it might really help Simone. It was a real rehab program after all. They helped people find the good in Texas and work for common goals. I couldn't make Simone see that, but I wasn't a professional. They could do it. They could change her mind.

"Hey Drew. You haven't sent the rehab list in yet have you."

"No it's right here. I was fixin' to take it over to city hall."

"Well I've got one more name to add."

"Ok Steve. You sure do keep them busy over there. Eyes like a Hawk."

HANK - 5
Langley, Virginia, USA

"For the last time." The man in the dark suit walked back around in front of me and placed both hands on the table. "Here's the bargain. You take it, you get a plea bargain and go free after the deal is done."

"I know, I heard it already." I was extremely weary after countless hours without sleep.

"Let me refresh, just in case you missed some points. I want to make very sure you understand, here. Ok? We get you a face-lift, new identity and papers. You return to Texas as a German businessman, ostensibly in the superconductor industry. Now that's big there and there's lots of German manufacturers so you'll have some sway without sticking out. Now, when you start making the deals, you drop hints about funneling some extra Euros their way. Certainly they could use them, even with the war winding down. This is very important information for the US, Hank. We get this nailed, the UN declares the government corrupt, we get the steward rights to their economy and they're back in the fold."

"That's a pipe dream. Texas hasn't cooperated with the UN from the beginning."

"Right, but they'll have to if they get caught in this, because Germany will dump them like a wet rag, ok? Now once they've chosen us as steward, as the lesser of two evils between us and the UN, because God forbid they let Mexico steward, we're back on top. Texas is the plug that stops the leak see. Ozarkia comes back, the MSA, the Great Plains the whole shebang and we concentrate on California and Chicago. Now if you're all against Texas, like you say, you should want to do this as a patriotic American. It shouldn't matter that it's your only chance. Either this or hard time, maybe worse. Treason's not real popular these days."

"But common."

"Well Hank, just sign here and save your life while doing your duty, ok?"

He put a pen and paper on the table in front of me for the fiftieth time.

"Listen sir. With all respect, I decline." I had it memorized by now. It had to annoy them a little that I repeated the same thing every time. "I will not bargain. I have done nothing wrong. Either you let me go to Colorado, or you wrongly punish me. Your choice."

The old guy steamed between the ears to hear that again. He could almost say it with me I'll bet. The routine broke before his usual admonitions and put-downs when a snot-nosed secretary came in with an arm full of papers.

"Is this Hank Connely?"

"Yeah. What do you want with him?" The dark suit man moved between the secretary and me.

"If you'll sign here, the director has released him on recognizance, to become academic adviser in London for the Colorado Academic Exchange Mission there."

"Oh give me a break. Let me see that." He grabbed the paper out of the secretary's hand.

In less than five minutes, I was on the phone with Jack Croslin who had worked a loophole that released me from treason by taking an academic post in London.

"It didn't hurt that Director Maori is an old student of mine. I helped her along in transferring to Harvard. She's bright and could live with transferring you out of the country, well, off the continent as they say now. Tight loophole but I got you through."

"Thanks Jack. I owe you big, again."

"You paid me back when you saved that guy John. That was brave Hank. Believe me it was. I think you're doing ok."

"How are Faye and Jeff?"

"Fine. I have to call them soon. Big news."

We talked a little more about old times and I hung up. I had fourteen hours to get my things together and head to National Airport and fly to London. I felt the same old surge of adrenaline I'd got in my political days. But it felt a lot better. That old heavy weight, the specter of Rich Morgan, seemed off my back for a while anyway. I practically jigged out the front door of Langley to catch my taxi.

Newcity of Chicago - 2

A man named Frank sat staring at the wall opposite the terminal. His life in war torn Chicago had become drab and uninteresting. The opposite of what he had thought when he stayed behind, so his roommates Gary and Bone could get away clean. After the initial excitement of the city's takeover, everything settled into the same old bureaucratic routine.

He'd heard from Bone a few times since then. She lived safely in Milwaukee. As safe as Milwaukee ever was. Frank was trapped in Chicago. His employment with the AAF government kept him safe but it also kept him there. He was free to stay in the city and move about it as he pleased but not free to go. He was too 'essential' as a customs agent.

Someone tapped him on the shoulder.

"Hi. We're trying to make a connecting flight to Denver." A young lady and a young man with a camera stood at the gate.

"Denver? What are you flying to Denver out of Chicago for?" Frank was suspicious.

The woman looked like she might fall asleep on her feet. The guy did the talking. "We're coming from Asheville."

"Ah got hijacked and rerouted." That made more sense .

"Yes, you know?"

"People going anywhere to the west generally have to come through Chicago at some point because they've been hijacked. It's how we make a lot of our money. Buy a hot dog or two while you're here, maybe they'll raise my salary."

"Don't you need to see my ID?"

"Why? You hiding something? Or is it an especially good fake you think I'll appreciate? I know. I bet it's pre-war. You're from where?"

The woman woke for a second. "Colorado."

"Cool, let me see it."

The guy produced his Colorado Driver's License. His name was Jeff.

"Wow, you have been away a while. They destroyed all these when the Texans invaded. All the new ones are really drab with this mountain thing and say Colorado Republic. We don't get to see too many real drivers' licenses from out west anymore. Damn."

"So can we go?" he pleaded.

"Yeah. Just don't take any drugs, guns or political propaganda harmful to the state and uh, buy some hot dogs."

They moved on as an old college friend Helen and some guy who wasn't Frank's friend Steve walked up.

The not Steve guy wore a harried expression. He was telling Helen that someone would be fine.

"I just think Simone doesn't need this at a time like this. And who knows what'll happen to him in El Paso. He can get himself into trouble really easily there. I suppose you can't fly down and get them with things the way they are but..." Helen trailed off.

"Well she can't very well leave her job now, and besides the UN is all over New Mexico, even if it is Texas. Steve will be fine." The guy turned pleadingly to Frank.

"Hi kids. Having a domestic entanglement? Sorry. Not allowed in the Newcity of Chicago. Do you have any fruit to declare?"

The guy didn't miss a beat. He felt in his pockets. "I have some fruit flavored gum."

"No joking sir. See the sign. You must be very serious. Are you serious? Do you have gum? If so I'll have to confiscate a piece."

He handed Frank a piece of gum as Helen finally looked up.

"Frank?" She had her open-mouthed stunned look on.

"Hi Helen." Frank smiled, enjoying not acting surprised.

"What are you doing here? Didn't you get out?" Her mouth still hung open even as she talked.

"No. Gary and Bone went up to Milwaukee. And, you know, there's some fun stuff to do there but I thought I'd hang around and catch on painting walls or being a customs man or something. So here I am."

"Wow. Well what do you want us to do?" Helen finally closed her mouth.

"Prepare to be shot."

"What?" Her mouth shot open again.

"Well, if you look like you're about to be shot in Chicago, it usually deters you from being shot, because they figure somebody already has you pegged, so they move on to pick fresh bait."

"I thought joking in an airport security terminal was against the law." The guy pointed to the sign.

"Here in progressive Chicago I can get away with it. Unless somebody superior to me decides it's bad, in which case I'll be severely punished but only for my own good. Now if YOU were to joke I could arrest you, seize all your possessions, declare you dead and make you my houseboy. Unless the security commander wanted you."

"Don't they monitor you at these stations?" The not Steve guy waved towards an assumed hidden camera.

"OH, yeah but my commander is used to it by now. He trusts my instincts. For some odd reason."

Helen impatiently started to push on the guy. "Ok Frank. Well, we're moving to Champaign for awhile. We should get together."

"Don't talk treason man. I can't abandon my post with the Newcity." Frank's voice lost all mirth. He looked dead into Helen's eyes.

"Well can I get your address and phone?"

"Yeah sure."

They exchanged addresses on the backs of ticket stubs and custom slips.

"By the way, didn't you used to tag along with Steve?" Frank looked at Helen.

"Yeah, he stayed behind with Simone in New Mexico."

"Oh."

There was an uncomfortable pause.

"Well, write us." Frank let them through the customs gate. "Drive safely. We'll miss you."

He got the feeling he wouldn't see them again. Helen seemed happier than she ever had with Steve. From what Frank knew of Helen, when she was happy she disappeared and left the world behind. He turned the radio back up and resumed staring at the walls.

"This is an American Unity Radio News Update. In New York, I'm Greg Whitney.

"The Presidents of The US, The United Midwestern States and Ozarkia, today submitted a request to the United Nations to negotiate an immediate settlement among the warring factions of the former US. This is an abrupt change for the US, which until now, insisted that all negotiations lead to reconstruction of the old US. However, pressure from the powerful Midwestern States seem to have forced the US to the bargaining table. Almost all the other republics and nations have announced agreement to this plan. Leaders will sit down with UN arbitrators in Vancouver to discuss a lasting peace. This has been an American Unity Radio update."

GEHRIG - 5
Greenville, Illinois

The house looked like a corpse. I could still recognize it but the life was gone. One light burned dimly in the front room. It looked like a candle.

I hadn't seen John since we got back. He said everything was fine, he just needed to be alone. Finally this morning, he'd called me and asked if I'd come over at six o'clock.

I looked at the porch where I'd first gained an inkling of the Ozarkian plans. It struck me odd that it didn't look different. With so many borders and lives entirely changed or ruined, this old porch hadn't budged or adapted a bit. It reminded me of stories I'd read of the French Riots of the 1800's. One street would have a barricade and Revolutionists exchanging grapeshot with National Guards. Two streets over carriages would shuttle people from house to house as business carried on as usual.

I knocked on the door and it swung open of its own accord. A large candle burned on the table in the front room, shedding a rather small light for such a great column of wax.

Next to the candle I found a note from John. Rather prosaic, this candle and note in the place of email and a light bulb. It didn't bode well and I shuddered to think what the note contained. The house had a gloomy air. As a criminologist, my training forced me to guess what such isolation, drama and gloom could mean. I didn't want to think. I didn't want to read the note. I'd lost too many for reasons outside of anyone's control. I couldn't bear the thought of losing another at their own hand.

I steeled my courage and opened the folded paper.

Dear Rob,

I know what you must think. Don't worry. I've gone to a better place but it's not heaven. (or hell). I couldn't take this place anymore. Certainly not this house. I would have met you in person, but circumstances prevented me from it. Perhaps it's dramatic, perhaps it's a little sadistic teasing, but I felt impelled to leave you this solemn note in its solemn surrounding.

I've emailed you the necessary information to dispose of my property for me. Please donate the money to the Ozarkian Guard's fund. They'll know how best to distribute it.

I'm not good with words like Mack was. I can't express how deeply I feel the pain of what's happened. It's changed me and I know what I'm about to say will worry you, but I want you to know it's for the best. I've thought about it very carefully. In the end, we all die and we never quite know why we're here.

Mack is dead and so am I. And so in a way I am killing myself but not in the way you think. I cannot tell you any more and I must ask you to burn this letter once you've read it. The candle will come in handy for that.

I am gone but not forever. If some day a strange name floats through your mail and asks to meet you for lunch at the McDonalds on I-70 that's no longer there, you'll know to go. Until then, my friend, think good thoughts for me. I will need them.

Love,

John

I crumpled the paper and threw it at the ground. I knew it wasn't my fault, but I felt somehow I could have prevented him from whatever rash act he was about to perform. I imagined he had joined one of the splinter groups of the Ozarkian Republic that still dreamed of overthrowing the Texans. You had to know the right people and make many inquiries to contact those groups, but he knew them. Any attempt I made to find him could expose him to extreme danger. I had taken a position as a consulting criminologist for the National Health Service of the United Midwestern States in the capital city of St. Louis. I was a government official not likely to be trusted.

I burned the paper as he asked but I did not feel at rest... or ok. I felt betrayed. I stormed out of the house leaving the candle to burn. I'd wait for that invitation and spend the rest of my wrath on him then.

JEFF - 10
Denver, Colorado

"Have we ever heard what happened to Hank Connely or John?" Faye shouted from the kitchen.

"Nothing about John but he has our addresses, so I'm sure he'll mail us when he gets hold of a Deskset."

"What about Hank?" she asked, as I sat down next to her on the couch eating an apple.

"Yeah, I did hear something, today."

"What? Tell me!" She shook me.

"Not much really. They took him to Washington for an espionage trial. They tried to get him to plea bargain but he wouldn't do it."

"Anything else?"

"No. I guess they're deciding whether to make him a scapegoat. Not the death penalty or anything outdated like that but maybe life."

"That poor guy."

"He was having a crisis Faye. He saw his way of redeeming himself, that's all."

"I know, it's just that--" The telephone rang interrupting her. I walked into the back room to answer it.

"Woohoo!" I shouted, running back into the front room a few minutes later.

"What?" Faye looked at me expectantly.

"I just got a call from Professor Croslin. Can you believe this guy? He brokered a release for Hank to go to London. The Director of the CIA is an old student of his."

"He does amaze me sometimes. Geez. Is he doing all right himself?"

"Not only is he alive and well in Colorado Springs, but he tracked down my submission and it's going to be published in one week. Can you believe that?!"

"All right!" Faye smiled and hugged me.

"And he secured an interview with American Belief or American Unity or whatever they are these days on their evening netcast."

"Oh my god!"

"I need a suit!" I ran off to our room.

"You need someone to puncture your big head." She ran after me down the hall.

MARSHALL EAGLE - 1
A Hilltop in Lakota

The sun glowed deeply and warmly in the west encompassing the sky behind Craig Eagle as he trudged up the hill of his ancestors. He made the pilgrimage four times a year, more if he felt events called for it. It helped keep him even and peaceful in times of great stress. Lately he had climbed the hill more frequently.

As he reached the top he let his mind float out over the expanse of the Lakota badlands, filling the empty space and joining the current of the world as it swept through the ravines and valleys.

Two Eagles danced in the air above him voicing a call of warning and triumph alternately.

He reached out to his floating consciousness and nudged it to flow over the events of the past few months, guiding it to a resolution of the many threads of life he encountered.

He looked northwest and smiled broadly. His two friends now comfortable and happy. He looked far to the east and smiled again at the troubled man who had overcome his biggest hurdle.

Then he let his gaze drift out in the direction of those unmet in person but still woven into the Earth. To the west he felt even and warm as he saw resolution but not triumph. Northeast he saw comfort at the price of complacency and felt pity. To the southeast he saw sorrow touched by madness and felt sad.

And finally as he faced south he saw anger, depravity, and hopelessness. Most of all he felt great despair. He shed a tear and prayed for the easing of troubles.

As the sun set, Marshall Eagle arose from the cold ground. His tour of the world from a hilltop showed him as it always showed him, the hope and necessity of working on.

KANDEL - 7
Los Angeles, California

It felt good to be back home. The California High Command gave me a big welcome back shindig and presented me with a new position, new salary, new car AND a penthouse apartment. Ok, so I'm a pig. So what? You'd turn it down? No way. Anyway, I sat in the back seat of my new black Saturn Kennedy talking on the phone, watching the familiar L.A. landscape drizzle past.

"Ok. Thanks General. Goodbye. Cameron? Send a notice to the Media Department that Bromberg and I are in full agreement on the I-10 management accord. Did you check on Steve and friends?"

"Yes sir. Helen and Mulu made it safely to Champaign and Simone is back home in the UN section of Las Cruces."

"What about Steve?"

"It seems he jumped a flight to El Paso at Benson and is now working for the Texas Department of Propaganda."

"In other words he flipped out. I knew it would come sooner or later. He always thought too much about stuff."

"Yes sir. Sounds like he flipped all right."

"Great. Oh. We're here."

I got out in front of the Hall of Justice to take care of some quick business. I felt kind of like a super hero actually. I half expected to find Superman and Aquaman waiting for me at the door. Cameron stayed in the car to wait for me. My office was non-governmental over in the new CPP building. I had been justly rewarded with the title of Diplomatic Chair of the Southwest. No longer would I have to dirty my fingers in actual politics. I would just sit in a cool office, in a nice comfy leather chair, barking orders out over the phone and taking long baths in my executive bathroom. But I had one last stop to make before embracing my new life.

I climbed the dark stairs to Stephanie's floor. As I approached her office, I heard her say, "Beer tonight?"

Another voice said, "Right." Then a tall blonde man walked out of her office and headed down the hall.

"Spoils of war?" I swaggered in, showing off my new suit.

"What?" Stephanie barked. I had surprised her in so many ways. I loved it.

"Nothing. Look, I wanted to see if you had some time to talk but I see you're busy." I turned to leave.

"Mark, don't be such a child."

I stopped and gave her as dangerous a look as I could muster.

"I..." I slowly approached her desk, "am," I put my hands down firmly on the desk and stared straight into her eyes, "ANYTHING but a child these days. Take your reaction formations somewhere else, Miss Pop Psychology. I have been through hell and returned. I've caused death and destruction and risked my life to prevent it. All to do a job I was sent on, to get me out of YOUR hair. You don't think I know that? You don't think I'm pissed? You don't think I may have changed just a little tiny bit?! I am NOT a CHILD," I yelled. "You could have just told me. We could have talked. Hell, we might have even worked it out. Maybe that's what you were afraid of. Well fine. If that's the way it's going to be I have other things to do. Important things."

I left her office for the last time.

"Mark!" she yelled.

STEVE - 15
Las Cruces, New Texas

The Deskset in the main room of the Texas Department of Propaganda blathered on about the 'peace' settlement while I tried to spin an article about life improvements in New Texas. It was hard. The natives here did everything they could to slow down progress but some advancements had been made. I paused to hear the outcome of the Vancouver Conference.

"We now go to Anna Lubov, in Vancouver, with the latest."

"Thank you Greg, the week is up and the results are few but momentous. UN chief Negotiator Raoul Mohammed announced the three parts of the settlement just minutes ago. We already told you of the first. The borders of Ozarkia were set south of Little Rock, meaning the Texas Army will have to withdraw from its recent siege position. Part two calls for all other borders to remain where they are. This provision became workable when a last-minute offensive by Colorado, completely freed Denver two days before the talks. The Colorado-Texas border would have been much trickier than Ozarkia. The third result is almost laughable in the face of the other issues. The United States demanded very vehemently that Pennsylvania and Eastern Ohio stop calling themselves the United States of America. The Pennsylvanians wouldn't budge and it wasn't resolved until this morning. Pennsylvania will now call itself the States of America or SA. A strange bargaining move but I think the US wanted to gain some feeling of influence. Native Americans in Arizona, who did not attend the meeting, will have to handle their complaint through the normal UN mechanism. Mr. Mohammed stated that for now, the Native American Communities will become independent protectorates under California and Texas."

"What about the Aryan Nation Anna?"

"Well, on the official map put up this morning, the Aryan Nation borders are drawn in but there is no country identification. The UN will not recognize them until they get assurances about human rights. Apparently it falls under the second part of the agreement but is effectively no man's land."

"The second part of the agreement meaning the freezing of all borders at present locations."

"That's right Greg."

"So this is not a painless settlement but as equitable as one would hope?"

"That seems to be the prevailing sentiment."

"Thanks Anna. So what is being called the Peace of Vancouver, puts to rest hundreds of years of history and begins a new tomorrow. I'm Greg Whitney, American Belief Radio News."

I decided to go up to the fifth floor. They had a set of classified private network Desksets there, in a room quaintly called, the 'computer room.' I wanted to find out what rehab center Simone had been assigned to. It took me awhile to find her file, because they'd classed it in a really weird way. Finally the results spat up.

```
Luna, Simone, 27
Warrant: TDP
Subversive

Assignment: Port Arthur Center MHMR

Deceased en route.
EOF
```

"What?!" An involuntary cry escaped my lips. "What's that mean?"

I called up my friend Joe at the Rehab Distribution Center.

"Yeah, that's right, Steve. The bus blew up on the way out of town. That happens a lot with the subversive buses. You know. Was she a relative or something?"

"No, just a friend."

"Well with friends like that, who needs enemies? Sorry Steve, but it's probably best. She would've just got you in trouble. See you later."

I felt nothing and I was scared. I'd killed her. But a digital death is so remote. She might still be out there like some piece of lost data. Bullshit. She's dead. Get it through your thick skull. The first thing to get through there since you left Helen. You didn't kill her but you didn't help any. Selfish fool. And you can't undo this one Steve. You can't go back and fix it. Can't redo the take. Can't call a Mulligan. It's done. Permanent. Destroyed in the fire.

I opened the window and looked down on Las Cruces... dammit, this was New Mexico not New Texas. Why did I fall for that? Why? It can't be. I can't let it happen. It's not right, but it's too late. I thought of Simone and began to cry. The hot wind dried my tears but not as fast as they were flowing now.

I hated Texas. Not the buildings or the people, but the heat. The hot crazy air drove you mad, drove you on, drove your best friend's bus into a fiery death. I looked down at the street below. My hate came back double force. I had been keeping it in check to hide my pain over Helen, but the pain over Simone dwarfed it and overcame my defenses. Helen had left. Simone was dead. My head became a swirl of hot coals against Richard Morgan and the whole damn mess of countries on this godforsaken continent.

I looked down at the dusty sidewalk below. Like the rest of the country, I had reached the boiling point. Boil over the edge, I thought. Boil over. And I did.

THE END

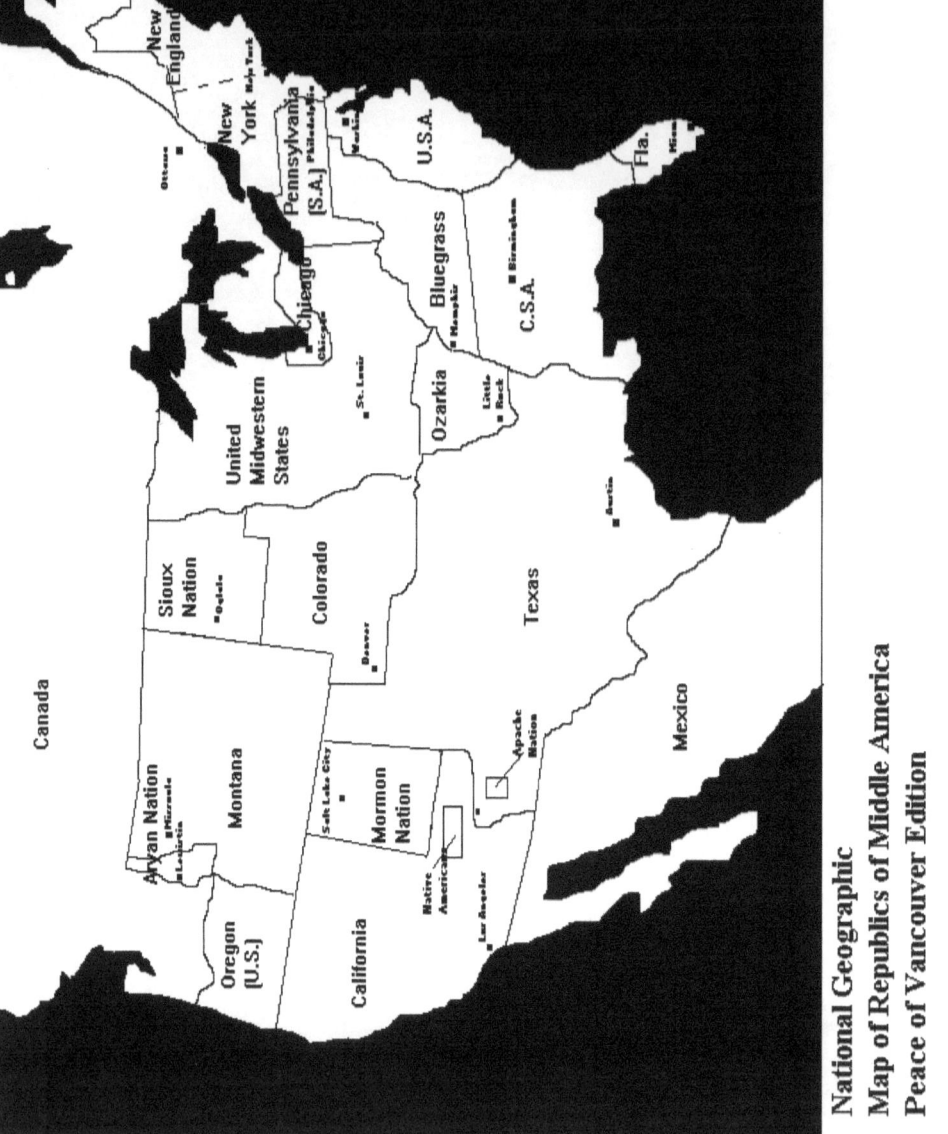

National Geographic
Map of Republics of Middle America
Peace of Vancouver Edition